PHOENIX RISING

PHOENIX RISING

The Elementalists
Book 1

Ephie & Celia Risho

PHOENIX RISING
The Elementalists, Book 1
Copyright © 2020 Ephie & Celia Risho.

This book is a work of fiction. Names, characters, businesses, organizations, places, events, and incidents either are the product of the authors' imagination or are used fictitiously. Any resemblance to actual persons, living or dead, events, or locales is entirely coincidental.

For more information: info@theelementalists.net.

Cover Illustration © Stephan Martiniere.
Developmental Editing/Line Editing: Ann Castro, AnnCastro Studio.
Inside illustrations, map, phoenix symbol: Olena Bushana.
Book & cover layout: Ephie Risho.
Fonts used in book: Desire Pro; Minion Pro.

Bozeman, Montana
ISBN (paperback): 978-1-7349741-0-2
ISBN (EPUB): 978-1-7349741-1-9
ISBN (hardcover) : 978-1-7349741-2-6
Library of Congress Control Number: 2020908478

First Edition

10 9 8 7 6 5 4 3 2 1

Dedication

Dedicated to the heroes who don't know that's what they are yet. May you find your path.

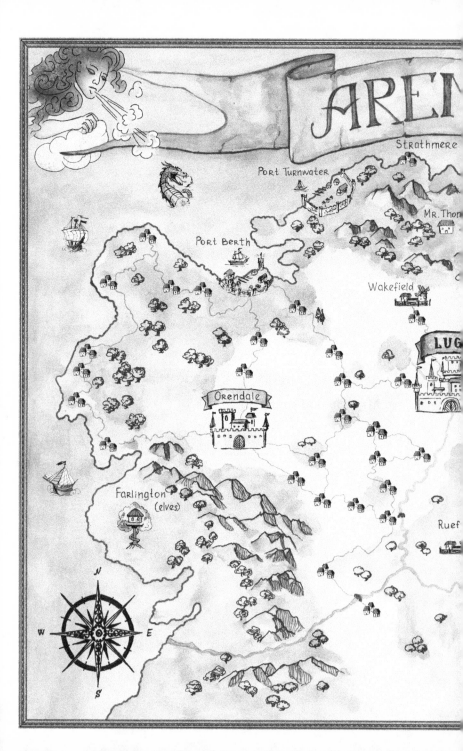

CONTENTS

Chapter 1 - Fields on Fire 11

Chapter 2 - Sabotage 21

Chapter 3 - Pixies 32

Chapter 4 - Escape 41

Chapter 5 - Old Mr. Thompson 49

Chapter 6 - A Bit of History 63

Chapter 7 - Danger in the Woods 76

Chapter 8 - New Friends 87

Chapter 9 - Pursuit of Pixies 96

Chapter 10 - A Better Plan 105

Chapter 11 - Search for a Wizard 118

Chapter 12 - The Courier's Search 141

Chapter 13 - The Lookout 152

Chapter 14 - Forming a Plan 173

Chapter 15 - Good Gifts 184

Chapter 16 - Castles 194

Chapter 17 - The Dark 207

Chapter 18 - Goblin Army 221

Chapter 19 - Underground 228

Chapter 20 - The Trouble with Trolls 242

Chapter 21 - The Volcano 250

Chapter 22 - Pixie Power 267

Chapter 23 - Phoenix Rising 279

Chapter 24 - A Bigger Library 292

Chapter 25 - Magical Strategies 304

Epilogue 318

About the Authors 321

Acknowledgments 323

Chapter 1

Fields on Fire

THE SMALL PIXIE LAUGHED DEEPLY, a full belly laugh that made Amber wonder how such a small creature could send her voice echoing through the woods.

"It's *supposed* to be like this!" She grinned and twirled the black-and-bright-yellow-striped hat her mother had just knitted. It certainly stood out from the woodland greens and browns around them. Amber shoved it on her head, then brushed a strand of wiry brown hair away from her eyes before stuffing it up under the hat.

"If I ever see you wear that in the forest, I'll be shocked." The pixie's high squeaky voice matched her smile.

"Yeah, not very practical. That's true." Amber twirled the stubborn strand of hair that fell back out. "So . . . you were going to tell me something important?"

"Was I?" The pixie flashed a mischievous smile.

The town bell faintly sounded in the distance. *Gong. Gong. Gong.* They both quieted. Amber tried to remember if there was an event or other celebration she might have forgotten. The young pixie stared at her with raised eyebrows, and Amber sighed. "I have to go. Be well, Flurry."

"You too." The little pixie darted up into the air as Amber turned and ran toward the town.

I hope it's nothing serious, she thought. Maybe it's just a wedding or something.

As she approached Seabrook, she picked up the pace, then paused near the first farm to catch her breath. The faint smell of smoke filled the air, and her heart broke. This wasn't the friendly smoke of a fireplace or backyard firepit. This was the smell of too much burning. Of wheat and other crops, perhaps.

She dashed to the city center where her friend Ryder was directing everyone who arrived. "The fire is on the Peabody's field! Hurry, before it spreads! It's gigantic!"

She panted with hands on knees and admired the teenager's leadership. He was about four years older, around sixteen, but so responsible. He'd been the town's courier since before he was Amber's age, so he was often far from their small hometown.

Ryder stood on the third step, next to a life-size statue of a heroic-looking man brandishing a sword. Young and old alike ran from all directions to the statue where Ryder was directing villagers toward the fields on the east side of town. He glanced down at her and pointed to the sea. "Amber! Get to the docks and let the fishermen know, so they can help when they arrive."

Amber immediately dashed to the cliffs that overlooked the great sea and the docks. The waves crashed into the rocks below, sending spray into her face. Fifteen small fishing boats splashed through the waves toward her, the men straining at their oars with intense energy. Some of the larger boats had their sails up, tacking back and forth in the slight spring breeze. The loud bell continued to ring out behind her sending chills through her body.

The boats began arriving, some of the smaller ones were rowed straight up the shoreline and tied to manmade knobs in the rocky cliffs. The larger ships pulled into the docks next to a few other boats.

"Hurry!" Amber waved and jumped. As the men ran up the stairs, she shouted above the roaring waves, "The

Peabody's fields! They're on fire!"

As each boat approached, she shouted and directed them where to go. The men quickly tied their boats and ran toward the burning fields. Some filled buckets with sea water and carefully walked toward the fire. Others just ran to get there as quickly as possible.

After the last boat landed and the three fishermen went to fill buckets, Amber sprinted toward the rising smoke plumes behind her village. She cut through Old Mr. Crabtree's barley fields and let out a cry when she felt the heat from the ravaging fire.

The flames were far more intense than anything she'd ever seen before, and looked like they could easily spread to the village.

Desperation was in everyone's eyes.

Amber's dad stood, completely covered in ash from head to toe, and pointed across the field. "The water tower!"

A dozen people ran toward the tower, situated next to two tall coastal redwood trees. Under her dad's direction, some brought over the largest wagon and a team of horses while two men clambered up to the top, tying thick ropes into rings. The ropes were then thrown up to two other volunteers who'd also climbed the trees. They looped the ropes over thick branches, just above the tower.

Eight men lifted the wagon so that it was directly in front of the tower while two others stood with axes ready at the front legs. At her dad's nod, they began chopping at the legs and the tower began to topple.

"Pull the ropes!" Amber's dad shouted. The men heaved the ropes, holding up the immense bucket just enough so it didn't completely tip over and lose all its water. But the bucket was so heavy, they began to slip. More men dashed to grab the ropes, and together they lowered the bucket onto the wagon. The wheels of the wagon creaked and groaned.

"Quickly! Toward the fire!"

But the horses struggled under the weight. Four more horses were rounded up and tethered to the other four. Finally, the wagon edged toward the fire, wheels wobbling dangerously.

Amber's dad shouted, "Wait! Not yet!"

Finally, the heat grew so intense that the horses refused to go any further. The men led the horses back, turning the wagon sideways toward the fire before grasping the ropes and heaving on them.

The bucket teetered, then toppled over, pouring water over the field and dousing the worst of the flames.

"Now! Shovels!" Men, women, and children ran toward the fire and began digging up dirt and heaving it onto the flames. Someone thrusted a shovel into Amber's hands, but she looked around desperately. Where should she start? The task seemed daunting. She saw her brothers and sister shoveling dirt onto the fire to her left. She ran over and joined them, straining under the burden before them.

A flame leaped toward her and she fell back, then gritted her teeth and tossed a shovelful of dirt onto it. It felt like the wheat was screaming in pain.

The grime on her lips tasted bitter, and her hands blistered from work they weren't used to doing. She felt her arms and back burn from the repetitive motion and desperately wanted a break but knew she couldn't.

Smoke filled her eyes, and she tried not to cry. She could hardly breathe, so she lifted her shirt to cover her mouth and nose, which helped a little bit. She wondered if she could keep going but imagined what would happen if the fire approached the town buildings.

We can't let it spread! she thought. An extra surge of strength stirred within her. She worked even harder, shoveling, covering flames, spreading the dirt around to cover more, and repeating.

She and her three siblings worked alongside another five villagers on one little section. Other people were spread out all over the field, working in natural clusters, focused on preventing the fire from spreading to the town. It looked hopeless.

Amber paused to take a breath and saw Ryder looking around, fresh to the scene with a shovel in his hand—the only person not completely black from ashes and dirt. She waved him over, and he ran to join them.

"We can do this!" he said, picking up where she'd left off. Amber nodded and took another breath. It may have felt impossible, but what else could they do? She focused on digging again, trying to cover the flames as fast as she could.

Ryder, it turned out, was more effective at putting out the flames than the others. Nobody—not even Amber—noticed in the frenzy of the fire that Ryder, in between shovels, made sweeping gestures with his hands that stirred the earth, causing it to move, roll over, and completely cover the flames.

Within a few minutes, what had felt like a daunting task suddenly seemed possible. Their little area was down to the last few flames, small and easy to extinguish. Amber paused and leaned on her shovel for a moment as other villagers covered the last of the flames.

She and her siblings looked around. The fires still raged on another part of the field, and Shane, Amber's oldest brother, shouted, "Over there!"

They ran across the field and started shoveling beside the other townsfolk.

After what felt like an eternity, the townspeople had put out the worst of the fire in the entire vicinity. They stopped their work, leaning on their shovels and taking stock of the situation.

With much of the fire doused by the water tank and all the hard work of the villagers, the remaining flames were smaller and more spread out. The people of the village were scattered, from the town all the way to the forest, chasing every fire that could cause trouble.

Amber took a deep breath. Her entire body was black with ashes and dirt, and her arms ached from constant digging, but she smiled. The fire was under control. They'd done it. The fire had only engulfed one field and not damaged any buildings.

Shane patted her on the back, sending black ashes flying into the air. "Nice work, buckaroo." He smiled, a white grin on an entirely blackened face.

Amber smiled back. "Thanks. You too."

"Hey, Ryder!" Amber's brother Patrick called. "Glad you could join us! It felt like we weren't going to tackle those flames until you showed up. You were just what we needed to tip the scales."

Ryder wiped his wands on his filthy pants, then chuckled when he realized they were even dirtier than before. "You bet. Doing my duty. I'm glad I happened to be here. I wasn't supposed to be back in town till tomorrow, but something told me to rush back."

"We're glad you made it, for sure." Kirsten, Amber's older sister patted his shoulder.

Amber nodded, too exhausted to talk. She watched the people wearily chasing the last of the fires. Her dad was nearby, leaning on a shovel and looking utterly exhausted. She walked over and gave him a big hug. "We did it."

He lightly stroked her tangled hair and smiled. They watched the others for a minute, and then he said thoughtfully, "This wasn't a normal fire. This was far worse—there's no way it started by natural means. It was sabotage. I'm certain of it."

He gazed into space and stroked his well-trimmed, soot-filled beard for a minute. "It begs the question: who . . . or what . . . on earth started this fire in the first place—and why?"

Chapter 2

Sabotage

THE GATHERING HALL was packed with people, every seat filled and townsfolk standing in every possible space, shoulder to shoulder. Although it was chilly outside, the doors were wide open to bring some fresh air into the crowded space. Five dogs played near the entrance, waiting for their owners.

Amber stood in the back behind a crowd who blocked her view of the five people standing on the raised stage. The banging of a wooden gavel pierced the noise from the front of the room, and the great hall quieted.

"This wasn't a natural fire," a man at the front began.

Amber felt a tug at her shirtsleeve and looked behind her. Thomas, a young curly-headed boy, motioned for her to go outside. Curious, she followed. He pointed toward the edge of the village to a small shape sparkling in the night air. "The pixies want to talk to you. Come on!"

Amber jogged after Thomas, past a few homes down the dirt road. Two other children joined them. They approached the woods and path they often took to visit the pixies. Flurry hovered at the tree line, looking finely dressed as always, which jarred with the worried expression on her face.

"Oh good. It's you, Amber."

"What is it? What brings you this close to the village, Flurry? I don't think I've ever seen you come this far before."

Flurry's eyes darted back and forth. "Come deeper into the trees first. I don't like being out here in the open."

Amber and the children looked around, then followed the pixie a bit farther into the woods. The forest was dark. Finding the path would have been harder without the slightly glowing pixie darting in front of them. A few minutes in, the pixie relaxed, then turned back to them.

"We think we're being attacked." She flitted about nervously and glanced into the shadows surrounding them.

Amber felt a chill run down her back. "What do you mean? Who would want to attack pixies?"

"This fire. It wasn't natural. Do you know what caused it yet?"

"No. We're discussing that right now."

Flurry looked serious. "Fires are very dangerous for us. And not just when they happen. If the forest is burned down, we can't live in it anymore. It's a big deal. That was a big fire. Like someone started it."

"I know. That's what they were saying. I'll know more soon."

"Hmm." The pixie frowned. "Fires are dangerous for you, of course. But we think someone's attacking us. Here's the thing." She sighed. "Something's not right in the woods. I don't know if we're going to stay. I'll tell you more, but not now." Her eyes darted around. "Listen, after you know more, talk to me, ok?"

"Yes. Absolutely." Amber nodded somberly. The three younger children next to her were quiet with serious expressions. "I'd better get back to the meeting."

"See you tomorrow morning, Amber." Flurry waved, then fluttered away, disappearing into the dark woods.

Amber and the children walked back to the gathering hall. As they approached, they could hear the voice of someone sounding rattled. Amber stood outside with the kids and listened.

"We all have to work together! We can't be caught unprepared."

The townsfolk murmured approval. "We'll divide up into three groups, with Denison, James, and Douglas leading them. If you're needed somewhere, we'll let you know. Now get a good rest, and let's come back tomorrow ready to get some work done. Meeting dismissed."

People began to walk out quietly with serious looks on their faces. Ryder was in a deep conversation with his dad when he saw Amber. "Heya, dreamer." He went back to talking with his father as they headed toward their small home down the street. She waited till her parents came out with her older siblings, then joined them on their walk back home.

"What did you talk about?"

Her mother held her hand. "There's talk that the fire was caused by some sort of creature. Douglas said he saw it—a flying beast—in the area when it began, like a giant red-and-orange flaming eagle the size of four cows. He also said it was headed into town when he shot at it."

Amber held her mother's hand more tightly. "What do *you* think it is, Dad?"

He spoke quietly, "Some say it's the phoenix come back. That does fit the description. But the phoenix from my grandfather's stories was friendly. It wouldn't have done something like this—it helped the folks of Seabrook over sixty years ago, if you recall, in the big fight against the trolls."

"Could it have been a dragon?" Amber asked.

"Doesn't fit the description. But possibly. Maybe a small dragon? One never knows with these things."

"I think it was a phoenix," her brother Patrick said. "I've read all the books on magical creatures, and it fits the description perfectly." As usual, he sounded smug.

"What do *you* know?" Shane asked with scorn. "Have you ever seen a phoenix?"

"No, but I've seen pictures and read about them in a number of different books. Unlike *some* people who don't read very much." He glared at his older brother. "Douglas's description fits the phoenix perfectly."

"Boys, this is not a good time to fight." Her dad placed a hand on Patrick's shoulder. "We're all in this together. We have a common enemy, and we need to figure out what it is."

They walked in silence for a moment, then Amber asked, "Did you talk about the pixies disappearing? I was just chatting with them today, and they didn't tell me anything in particular. But they're definitely sounding worried."

"Yes," Kirsten said. "I mentioned it." She looked at her brothers. "Because *someone* has to be useful around here."

Her brothers both rolled their eyes, and Patrick said, "Good grief. As if pixies disappearing is the biggest issue we need to talk about. What about the goblins?"

"Goblins?" Amber suddenly felt a chill run down her spine. "What about goblins?" She squeezed her mom's hand again.

"Yeah," Patrick replied. "Five of them. Green and nasty, all decked out in weapons and ready for a fight. I guess they killed Roger's best cow, and he tried to shoot them with a bow. But you know Roger, he can't hit anything. They took the cow and left, but Roger thinks they'll come right back."

"When did that happen?" Amber asked. "How come he never said anything?"

"Well, it happened yesterday," Patrick said. "And Roger's had his hands full—he was actually going to head to Wakefield today but decided not to. Ryder says other villages more inland are seeing goblins too. He says the roads are becoming less safe all the time."

"Roger says the goblins are probably close by, so be careful going into the woods." Shane looked at Amber with raised eyebrows.

"Who cares about Roger and a few goblins anyways?" Patrick asked impatiently. "I'm more interested in the phoenix. You know, Douglas said it was all fiery and headed toward the village when he shot at it and it turned toward him. He said it was hard to know what it was 'cause it was like a winged ball of flame, but it had these piercing bright eyes. When he shot at it again, it turned and left. I think it'll be back, and we should be ready to fight."

Kirsten chimed in, "He said it went east, along the coast."

"Whatever." Patrick shook his head and kicked a rock down the dirt road. "It's scary, and we need to be ready to shoot at it again."

Amber turned to her father. "Dad, what do you think? Why is all of this happening?"

"Good question. I don't really see any connection, except that it's all happening at once. The pixies are interesting. You said you talked with them?"

"Yeah. But you have to kind of trick them into saying anything. They never come out right out and say what's on their mind. It makes them feel more special and important, I guess."

Her mind raced. *I bet Flurry will know more about the goblins and the flying fire creature. She sure seemed upset tonight.*

They walked for a while longer, then approached the familiar green door of their small yellow house. A thin brown dog stood and wagged its tail when it saw them.

"What's our plan then? I heard that there are three groups and that you're leading one of them, Dad."

"Well . . ." Shane began.

"I'm going to practice my sword-fighting skills," Patrick interrupted. "And archery, of course, though I don't need much help with *that*." He looked at his older brother slyly. "Since I won the competition this year and all."

Shane shook his head. "Whatever. You're good, but you got lucky. It could have gone any of three ways, if you ask me."

"Nobody asked you, did they?" Patrick gave Shane a slight push.

Kirsten said, "I think we all should get more prepared, like we talked about at the meeting. Not just fighting—but be ready."

"Indeed," their dad said, heading to put a log on the fire as everyone else took off their shoes and hung their jackets. "At this point, we're going to set up watches in the town's lookout tower and in the lighthouse tower. We'll have people taking turns doing watches, and we'll all pitch in to help, so at least we can be ready for whatever comes next. But some folks are going to have to rebuild what's been destroyed, and there's talk about what sort of preparations to do if goblins come back."

"All townsfolk are going to be trained in some form of self-defense. You're good with a bow already, Amber, so I'm not worried about you." He looked at the other kids. "We've taught all of you to take care of yourselves, and none of you is lacking in your marksmanship. But there are lots of folks who are absolutely not prepared whatsoever. Everyone's going to be busy for a while, taking watch, learning combat techniques, practicing with bows and close combat weapons."

Amber frowned. "But, Dad, shouldn't we find out more about what's happening? I know you want people to be trained, but it seems like there's a lot going on out *there*. Don't you think we need to get out and do something? Find out more?"

Pacing back and forth, she clasped her hands together. "You've always told us to never wait around for things to come to us but to go out and make life happen. Why are we just waiting for the next trouble?"

"My thoughts exactly," Patrick said. "That's why *I'm* going to practice my hand-to-hand combat techniques and go find some goblins."

Kirsten smacked her forehead. "For goodness sake. What good is that going to do? You can be such a bonehead sometimes."

"It's more than I've heard you talk about," Patrick said. "You're just going to sit here and watch in a tower. Whoop-de-doo. Not for me. I'm going to get out there and find some goblins to put in their place."

Her dad shook his head. "You're both right. Patrick, we do need to send people around the village to ensure goblins don't come close enough to kill our flocks or—heaven forbid—any people. And, Kirsten, we absolutely need people on watch for any other flying creatures coming our way. If Douglas could scare it off with a few shots, that gives me hope that we can keep it at bay if we know it's coming."

"As for us older folks . . ." He looked at Shane. "There will be lots of rebuilding to do and work needs to be done to fortify our meager defenses. We could improve the wall that was begun twenty years ago—actually finish it—which would leave only a few ways to get into town. That would help a lot, I think."

"But someone still has to do the chores," Patrick looked at Amber. "Why don't you stay out of our way and make sure things still get done. Someone has to."

Amber sat quietly, a quiet frustration bubbling up inside. She tapped her foot on the floor and gazed into the fire. None of the answers gave enough of a clue. She wanted to know more, like why were all these things happening at once? It seemed too odd to be a coincidence.

Tomorrow, she thought. Tomorrow when I go back to the pixies, I'll tell them what I know and see what else I can learn. There has to be more we can do. Flurry was going to tell me something else today. I need to know what it is.

Chapter 3

Pixies

AMBER QUIETLY WALKED IN THE WOODS with an arrow notched at her bow. She was usually at peace in the old forest, as if she and the trees were good friends, like she understood them. But this time was different. The woods felt more ominous knowing goblins could be nearby.

"Flurry?" Amber called, walking up to the spot where they had often met in the past. She waited in the silence. Something was definitely not right. "Flurry?"

She peered into the trees. Was that movement? There was a flitter and a rustling. She strained to see. Suddenly a pixie went hurtling past branches in the distance, chased by a small, dark, flying imp. The imp looked evil and disgusting, with long dangly limbs and awful-looking talons on the ends of its fingers and toes.

She raised her bow and shot, missing by mere inches. The imp caught up with the pixie and snatched it out of the air with its long talons.

Her heart quickened.

She drew another arrow and shot. It landed in the imp's body, sending the creature to the ground.

She heard it thud in the distance and ran over to look.

The imp was definitely dead, but the pixie appeared dead as well. Amber immediately recognized him. He was Wix, a friend of Flurry's—a handsome pixie, who always made her smile. Tears welled up as she looked at his still face. Just as she reached down to pick him up from the imp's grasp, she had an eerie feeling there was another imp watching her.

She whirled around, her bow at the ready, and scanned the trees. She didn't see anything but sensed the forest wasn't at peace . . . an unwanted visitor was still there. She breathed in deeply, determining where the imp might be. A sudden prickly feeling trailed down the back of her neck, and she turned to look at a tall, old oak tree. She raised her bow, eyeing every branch.

A slight movement about twenty-five feet up caught her eye. She wasn't quite sure if something was there. The branch appeared to have something a bit dark on it. Was it moss? She aimed and released an arrow at the dark spot. The arrow whizzed toward it and thunked into something.

There was a high-pitched gurgle, then an imp dropped off the branch, knocking into a few other branches before falling to the ground. Amber stood waiting with another arrow notched. She listened and watched carefully.

Her mind raced. What did Mrs. Juniper teach me about imps? Think, Amber! Think! Do they travel in larger groups—or is this it?

She stood quietly for a few minutes, waiting. When she heard a bird chittering nearby, she relaxed.

"Flurry? Are you there? I think it's safe now." Her ears pricked, listening for any noise in the old forest.

After a moment she walked back to where Wix lay in the imp's talons. She picked him up gently, not disturbing his fragile wings. "Wix didn't make it. I'm so sorry. I wish I'd come sooner."

She caught a glimmer from the corner of her eye. Flurry and another fairy she didn't recognize fluttered toward her, eyes darting about anxiously. Flurry looked anguished when she saw her injured friend in Amber's hand.

"I'm so sorry, Flurry. I couldn't save him." Amber frowned and held out Wix. The fairy next to Flurry was an older male, dressed elegantly and looking confident. He flew over to Wix and lifted a small wand, waving it gently over the limp pixie. Amber watched in awe as Wix took a rugged breath.

"Not dead," the fairy said. "But very nearly. Thank you for saving him."

Amber breathed a huge sigh of relief. "Oh, I'm so glad. I thought for sure he was dead."

She turned to Flurry. "Is this why you pixies are leaving? Because you're being attacked?"

"So many questions." Flurry was instantly full of her usual spunky energy. She was dressed smartly in a blue-and-white tight-fitting outfit, which seemed quite out of place with the trauma they had just been through. In typical pixie fashion, she avoided Amber's question completely. "Here's what *I* want to know. Where's your new hat?"

Amber laughed. "Okay, you got me. You were right. But seriously." She looked at Flurry with pleading eyes. "You're obviously under attack. And we've learned more about the fire. It was created from a flying creature—we think it was a phoenix that attacked our wheat fields. Our whole town could have burned, and it looked like it was going to burn more things until someone shot at it. This seems pretty serious. Can you give me a hint about what's going on?"

Flurry looked at Amber, and her eyes softened. She was quiet for a moment, then said. "Thank you for saving Wix. Yes, we are leaving. At least for now. You should probably leave as well. I think you'll be able to help your village more out there." She pointed, and Amber turned to look into the woods before realizing Flurry wasn't pointing at anything in particular. Or was she?

Amber puzzled over Flurry's words. In some ways, she was surprised by the answer, but she also expected that any information she'd get would be unusual and hard to decipher. As a general rule, pixies were notorious for never giving away anything unless absolutely necessary. Amber had learned over the years that to get them to share anything meaningful she either had to make them think she already knew about it or give them significant compliments.

She had a theory that pixies actually traveled far and wide. That—combined with their habit to gossip—made them highly aware of happenings all over. But they rarely parted with information unless they felt it benefited them.

The pixie she didn't recognize helped Wix stand and supported him as he flew off Amber's hand. "I'm going to take him to Maple," he said, and the two fluttered into the woods. Wix flew slowly and erratically, and Amber's heart sank as she imagined the pain he was still in.

She turned back to Flurry. "You think I could do something out there? What would I do? I mean, I was thinking someone should find out more, not just stay here. But where would I go?"

"I want to give you something. Follow me." Flurry flew deeper into the woods, and Amber followed closely behind. She felt a slight exhilaration. Flurry had never shown her anything before. Was she going to see their home for the first time?

The two wound through trees and entered a small grassy clearing surrounded by tall trees. The place didn't feel unusual, although Amber was fairly certain she'd never been there before. She looked around, wondering if there was any clue about the place and realized it was completely ringed by yellow-and-orange mushrooms. She wouldn't have noticed unless she was looking for it. Was she in the pixie's home?

Flurry went to a hole in a large tree and flew inside, coming out a moment later with a sack draped over her shoulder. She carried it to Amber. "Put your hand out."

Amber put her hand out, and Flurry dropped the sack into it. It was about the size of a small coin pouch and had only one item in it.

"Open it."

Amber pulled out a smooth white rock with a black line notched on one side; it dangled from a string that went through the center of it. She glided her fingers across its smooth surface, then lifted the string and watched it spin around.

"It's an enchanted stone. Ask it where to go, and it will spin and point there. But you can only ask it one question, so be careful what you say. Don't use it unless you have to. After you invoke the magic, it'll always point in the right direction every time you pull it out. Try your best without it first."

Amber's heart pounded with excitement. A magical stone! She'd read about magical items in her books, but this was the real thing. She wasn't sure if anyone in Seabrook had anything enchanted. Was she the first?

"I don't know what to say, Flurry. Thank you. Thank you so much."

"No. Thank *you*. For saving us from those imps. And also for what you're about to do. I've appreciated our friendship, Amber. You should know you're special."

Amber looked at the pixie, puzzled. What does that mean? she wondered. She waited for Flurry to continue, but the pixie remained quiet.

"Um. So . . . how am I special?" Amber asked.

Flurry smiled. "It's your hat!" She had her usual mischievous smile again and flew back and forth in a jittery pattern that made Amber a little dizzy. It's what Flurry did when she was feeling excited. Amber giggled, and Flurry continued, "Maybe we'll see each other again. If all goes well, that will be soon! But I have to go now. They're waiting for me."

"Ok then." She tried to sound like it was all good, like not knowing didn't matter. But it did. A lot. Inside, she was anything but calm. Her stomach felt like it would explode. The pixies were always so difficult to understand.

Her thoughts swirled. What does that mean—I'm special? Special in a general way, like everyone is "special," or did she mean something more? I wish the pixies didn't talk in riddles! Still, she definitely gave me more information than usual. And the enchanted stone! I guess that means I should really go. But where? I suppose I can ask the stone if I get stuck.

She took a deep breath. "Alright then. That's it," she said out loud to no one. "I'll do it. I'm going to find out what's going on—why a phoenix would burn our fields and why the imps and goblins are attacking. I'll leave today. And nobody is going to talk me out of it!"

Chapter 4

Escape

FLURRY FOLLOWED HER FRIENDS through the forest, fluttering from tree to tree in case any other imps were out there.

I can't believe we're leaving our home of all these years, she thought. Wix and the elder who'd shown up from another tribe were far ahead of her, but she could sense their trail. She was only a few minutes behind them.

Maybe that's how the imps found us so easily, she wondered. Can they sense us like we sense each other? No, that's impossible. Only pixies have that ability . . . as far as I know.

Flurry frowned with the uncertainty as she rounded a familiar grove of ancient trees and looked at them wistfully. Who knew when she'd see them again? She had many great memories playing there when she was younger.

The sense of the other pixies grew stronger, and Flurry veered right, toward the sea. As she approached some large trees, she suddenly swerved straight toward them and disappeared into a tiny crack in the bark, entering into a large chamber with dozens of pixies inside.

The elder was laying Wix onto a cot, and another pixie was moving around him busily, wrapping his injuries and fussing about.

Wix saw her and gave her a weak smile. At least they'd survived those two imps, thanks to Amber. Imps were one of the scariest things to a pixie. Larger creatures were too slow and clumsy to navigate the trees, and forest creatures were always quick to help. Only a smaller creature with the ability to fly and maneuver through branches could even come close. More importantly, imps seemed to be resistant to direct attacks from magic. And after the events of the day, it appeared they were excellent at tracking down pixies.

Flurry found herself relaxing for the first time that day. They were definitely safe in this place. But what were they going to do next?

As if on cue, one of the elders fluttered above the others, raised her hands, and mind-spoke to them all: *Peace, my brothers and sisters.*

It was Molina, one of the wisest and bravest of her tribe. She floated gracefully in her neatly tailored white outfit, with hair nearly as white and a peace about her as if nothing were out of the ordinary. When the chamber quieted, she spoke out loud, "We have reason to believe the fires were caused by a phoenix. Our sister tribe has sent word." She nodded to the elder pixie helping with Wix, and he nodded back.

"Which brings us to the conclusion that someone—or some *thing*—is attempting to hurt us. The imps' attack this morning is another sign. We must continue west toward the other tribes and warn them."

A young man spoke up. "We need the power of the Tower—the Great Stone Tower! We need to see who's doing this."

The other pixies murmured among themselves, and Molina spoke again. "We very well may. But first, we must use our own means. We are far from the Tower, and there is plenty of power among us, if we use it wisely."

The pixies all nodded in consent. This was quite true. All of the four dozen pixies present knew magic in one form or another, even if just to set up a protective ring.

"We can be a formidable bunch. But we must be prepared. We can't be taken off guard again. Or we may suffer a true loss." She looked at Wix, who furrowed his eyebrows and nodded.

"Don't worry about our home. If we can learn what's happening and aid our other brothers and sisters, we may be able to return soon."

The room was quiet for a moment, then a young pixie asked, "When should we go? Is it urgent?"

"Let's leave in the morning, at first light," Molina said. "For now, let's rest and assess what we know. Anyone who has any information, please bring it to the elders, and we will discuss and make plans." At that, she wiped her hands, which was the pixie way of saying the conversation had ended. All the other pixies in the room went back to talking with one another, and Flurry flew over to Wix.

"How are you feeling?"

"Glorious." Wix flashed a wry smile.

Flurry laughed, then grew serious. "You nearly died."

Wix gently patted his bandaged side. "This? It's nothing. A story for my grandkids one day."

"Did you see where the imps came from?"

"Naw. They seemed to come out of nowhere. I tried a charm spell when I saw them, but of course that didn't work.

I guess it was just instinct to try it. Too bad they weren't lower to the ground, so you could've taken care of them."

"Yes, too bad." Flurry rubbed her fingers together in thought. "Amber asked some good questions this morning. I feel we're being targeted. Think about it. We've heard of other pixies leaving their homes from attacks, not just us. And imps! We haven't had imp attacks my entire life."

Wix chuckled. "Well, Flurry, you're only, what, fourteen? That's not a lot of years."

"True. But I think it's been a long time, that's all I'm saying. And now there are goblins, imps, and an attacking phoenix." She wrung her hands together nervously. "Something's going on. Aren't you scared?"

"I'm sure the elders will know what to do. We've been through a lot, but we always make it. Always. If the outside world knew the full potential of pixies . . . well, let's just say we've got a lot going in our favor. I'm not worried."

✴ ✴ ✴

Flurry tried to be calm like Wix, but she couldn't stop worrying and barely slept.

When dawn came, the elders mind-spoke: *It's time. Gather your belongings.* Flurry rubbed her eyes. It felt too early.

They left quickly without speaking, occasionally communicating to one another with their minds but staying as quiet as possible in case other imps were nearby. Scouts went out in all four directions. The pixies flew as one eastward, toward the next pixie village. After a little while, the scouts began returning with news—no imps found.

All felt safe, but the fourth scout still hadn't returned, and Flurry sensed a strange tingling worry. Wix and other pixies would always tell her she worried too much. This time was no exception. She suddenly had a deep fear that the scout wasn't going to return . . . that an imp was on their trail.

She looked around at the other pixies. They were mostly calm, as if they weren't on an escape mission. A couple kept glancing over their shoulders, though, and it encouraged Flurry that maybe she wasn't the only one concerned. Following her hunch, she flew behind a tree and hid in some bushy leaves, waiting and watching behind them.

She stayed there for a bit, breathing far too loudly.

Am I just being overly worried? I'll only stay a few more minutes . . . I don't want to lose the group.

Her breathing quieted, and she listened.

Was that a flutter?

She peered toward the trees where the sound came from. A flit of black jumped from tree to tree. An imp! She was right, but that didn't make her feel any better. What could she do? She had to warn the others, but if she moved, she could be seen. Imps have amazing vision—even better than eagles.

She thought of her options. She could try to sneak back to the group close enough to mind-speak to them. Or she could lure it away, perhaps. Or maybe wait till it passed, then sneak up on it. But then what? Her powers would need it to be close to the ground. How could she do that? Without getting killed, that is.

The imp flitted past her without noticing her hiding spot. Well, she thought, it's too late to lure it away. I need to stop it before it gets to the group.

The dark creature disappeared into the woods. Flurry took a deep breath. It's now or never. I can do this. Just need to be careful.

In an instant, she sped off toward the imp. But when she got nearer, the imp abruptly turned and pursued her. Flurry panicked and dove to the ground.

The imp followed with breakneck speed. Her plan suddenly seemed foolish.

She hurtled toward the hollow log she'd seen earlier and went straight into it, with the imp almost upon her. In an instant, she flew out of a side hole and turned, twisting her arms. The earth rippled, and the hollowed log went flying into a nearby boulder, cracking into hundreds of pieces.

The imp spiraled upward then plummeted onto some rocks and lay motionless. Flurry flew over to it, hovering and frowning. As she turned her hands over, the earth and stones surrounding the imp moved, piling on top of the creature. The imp started to sink into the ground, and in less than a minute, it was swallowed up. There was no sign of it anywhere.

She took a deep breath and listened to the woods for a moment, lost in thought. That was close. Too close. They're so fast—and dangerous.

She talked through options as she sped off toward the group: "They definitely have a way of tracking us. We have to have a better plan. I need to talk with the elders! We need to know what's going on, and quickly. I hope Amber finds something out. Soon. There's no time to lose."

Chapter 5

Old Mr. Thompson

THE WHOLE WAY HOME AMBER STRUGGLED. Even though she was convinced she would go, she felt way too unprepared to head out all by herself, with all the danger. But on the other hand, she knew deep down that *someone* had to figure out what was going on, or it would just get worse.

Part of her, too, felt like showing Patrick a thing or two. "Chores!" she argued aloud with herself. "All he thinks I'm good for is chores? Sure, I doubt anyone will take care of my plants properly. But still. I can do more than that! Just because I'm the youngest doesn't mean I need to sit back and watch. They'll see."

When she arrived home, she started packing. But it was hard to figure out what to bring. Was it for a few days or a month? Could she really be away from home that long? And how sure was she, really?

Every time her confidence wavered, she remembered why she was doing it. Nobody else was going to figure out why everything was happening. Besides, Flurry thought she was special somehow—that she was the person to do it.

She packed some food and clothing in the saddlebags on her golden horse, Buttercup. Their dog looked up at her with sad eyes, as if he knew she would be gone a long time.

She laughed and patted him on the head. "Oh Scrawny. You'll be fine without me." She began tightening the straps on the horse when her mother came in.

"Out for a ride? Are you sure that's a good idea with goblins in the area?"

Amber paused. She didn't want to lie to her mother but didn't want her mother to stop her either. Tension filled the horse stall.

"Don't stop me. I'm going."

Her mother nodded. "I know, dear." There was a glimmer of understanding in her mother's eyes.

Amber suddenly felt like crying and blinked away the tears. "I have to. We need to know what's going on. And we can't all wait around here for the next attack. What if it only gets worse? I'm not going to stay around here and let that happen."

"No. Nor should you. You need to find out for yourself what's going on."

"You're not mad?"

"Why would I be?" Her mother smiled gently. "I was just like you at your age. Wanting to get out and change the world." She looked over at Amber's horse, laden down with supplies. "Do you have a plan?"

Amber looked down and didn't reply.

"Well, Old Mr. Thompson is a good start. He knows a good many things and has advised our village through some difficult times in the past. Also, I know Ryder will be headed out that way today, and he could probably ride with you, to get you started."

Amber nodded. "Thanks, Mom. That's a great idea."

Her mother's eyes twinkled. "Now let's make sure you have enough things packed."

She spent the rest of the morning helping Amber, making sure she had enough food, proper bedding, healing herbs, a canopy for rain, a pouch filled with flint and steel, and even some fishing gear. "There will be plenty of creeks and rivers. Lots of opportunity to fish!" she said.

Amber packed, partly excited but also scared. She felt like changing her mind when she got a sense that her mother was fretting or nervous. But her mom continued to pack and act like the decision was final, which gave Amber a boost of confidence.

It wasn't until Buttercup was fully loaded down with three days of food that her mother finally said, "I also brought you this." She held up a book before carefully putting it in one of the saddlebags. It was Amber's favorite book—she'd read it a dozen times—a story about elves, dragons, and adventure. She smiled and gave her mom a huge hug.

She wasn't entirely sure why she loved the book so much. They had other books that drew her interest as well. But her mom had mentioned at one point that her ancestors were involved in heroic stories like those in that book, and it got her thinking that maybe one day she might be a hero too. Of course, it was just a dream, never something she thought she'd actually do.

"And this." Her mom held out a small silver medallion on a chain. It had an intricate sun with a face etched on it.

"What is it?"

"Oh, an old family keepsake. It'll bring you luck." She undid the clasp and put it around Amber's neck. "It goes back a long way, I don't know how long, but I know at least to your great-great-great grandmother."

"Whoa. That's a lot of greats! I bet she's great." Amber winked at her mom.

Her mother chuckled and gave her a huge hug. They stood for a moment, then her mother wiped a tiny tear. "I know you're in a rush, but say goodbye to your dad. He'll be in Mr. Peabody's fields. Ok. Off you go, my brave little girl."

Amber mounted Buttercup, then grinned at her mom as she put the black-and-bright-yellow wool hat on her head. "Don't worry, Mom. I'll prove you right. I'll figure out what's happening and then come back to help." She gave a little kick with her heels and set off down the street. Looking back, she saw her mom's face, moist with tears but also beaming a warm smile. Amber knew deep down that her mom wanted her to go—but not really.

She found Ryder in the town center. He was waiting for any latecomers with mail for Lugo—a large city far from their tiny village, a two day's ride away.

She waved brightly. "Hi, Ryder. I hear you're heading out soon."

"That's right." He looked at the gear on her horse with raised eyebrows. "And something tells me you aren't here to pass me mail to deliver."

Amber grinned. "Now what gives you *that* impression?"

Ryder laughed. "Where are you off to?"

"I don't know. But I'm starting with Mr. Thompson."

"Perfect," Ryder said. "Not far at all. I can ride there with you. We can leave whenever you want. I was just about to call it quits."

"Sounds good. I just want to pass by the Peabody's field, if that's ok with you."

Ryder nodded and mounted Rocky, his splotchy white-and-brown horse with a long lightning pattern on its right side. Amber trotted next to him, and the two rode through the streets till they came to the field, which was still smoking from the fire the day before. Her dad and others were busy reclaiming what they could from the devastation.

She dismounted and walked over to him awkwardly. "Hi, Dad."

He looked at her, then at the horses and Ryder, and then looked into her eyes with understanding. "I see. Does Mom approve?"

"Yes." Amber tried hard not to look down. "I'm starting with Mr. Thompson, and I'll send word when I know more."

Her dad put his hand gently on her shoulder. "Somehow I always knew you'd be the one to head out first. Patrick might head out as well. But you . . . one thing I should tell you before you go. Amber, we have some great heroes in our family history, as we've told you before. Just remember, there are some folks out there who live a lot longer than we humans. I wish I knew more, but your mother's side played an important role long ago in the great wars. If you ever hear stories about Majestic Rose, that's someone you're related to."

"Anyway," he pulled her in for a hug. "I'll miss you. Be smart. Be safe. And send word when you learn anything."

Amber nodded, then walked back to Buttercup. "Let's go."

Ryder kicked in his heels, and the horses clopped onto the small dirt road that led through the countryside.

"You must love traveling these roads, since you're still doing it after all these years," Amber said.

"Oh yes. I think it's the adventure of it. I was eleven when I started, so young, and I ran into all sorts of interesting things."

"Really?" Amber asked. "Like what?"

"Well, in Seabrook things get interesting when someone catches a large fish or when a visitor comes to town. Except for yesterday," Ryder said as an aside. "But in larger towns, there's a lot more going on. There are people from all around the world. People who look and talk differently than we do."

"Such as?"

"Well, did you know not everyone is fair skinned, like the folks of Seabrook? I've seen people who are as black as the night. And I've seen some different races as well. Like elves."

"Elves. Mom says our family had elf friends in the past."

"Really?" Ryder gazed at her curiously. "I wonder how long ago."

"I don't know. But you said you had some adventures?"

"Oh yeah. Most exciting—I had some bandits try to rob me once."

"What?" Amber's mouth dropped open. "What did you do?"

"Well, it's kind of hard to explain . . ." He stared into the distance.

"You can't leave it at that! It was just getting good!"

"Ok. Ok." Ryder looked around nervously. "I haven't really told people about this before."

Amber excitedly twirled on a hair strand that had come out from under her hat.

"So I was all worried and excited when all of a sudden there was an earthquake and the ground gave way beneath the bandits. They fell down—and that gave me time to mount Rocky and ride off as fast as I could go."

"Wow, that's crazy."

"Yeah," Ryder said. "Definitely crazy."

They rode in silence for a moment. "Do you think it was a coincidence or magic?"

"Oh, it was magic. Definitely. In fact . . ." He gazed into the distance, "I know I caused it."

Amber paused. "Can you still do stuff like that? Can you do magic?" She thought of the book in her side bag, and the magic that was possible in her stories. Not just stories, she thought, as she patted the enchanted stone in her pocket.

"Sort of. Big stuff like that seems to be tougher, and only when I'm scared, that sort of thing. But yeah, look at this."

He waved his hand, and the rocky road flattened itself out. Pebbles sank in, larger rocks rolled into dips, and the earth rose up to match it. In a matter of seconds, the bumpy road was transformed. "Definitely useful when you're traveling a lot of roads in bad shape."

"How long have you been able to do this?" Amber stared at the perfectly flat road with fascination.

"Well, I figured it out with the bandits, like I said. That was two years ago. And I've been practicing with it ever since."

"Amazing." She gazed at Ryder with new admiration. "Tell me another story."

"Ok. Well, I ran into a huge wild cat once. Like, not normal size at all."

"Were you on your horse?"

"Yeah. So I felt sort of safe. But even so, it was *big*. Like bigger than any cat I've ever heard about."

"How big?" Amber asked.

"Oh, gosh, almost as big as Rocky here."

"That *is* big. What did it do?"

"Nothing—except scare me and Rocky out of our wits. It's amazing we're still alive, honestly. I bet it could have shredded us for breakfast if it had wanted to."

"It just stared at you?"

"Yeah. Like it was smart or something. I was so scared, but I also kind of knew it wasn't going to hurt us. The way it looked at me with its eyes, like it was thinking."

"Huh." Amber gazed at the leafy trees as they passed. "I always wondered why you decided to become a courier, especially so young."

Ryder looked down. "You know how my mom suffered so much before she died . . ."

"Yeah, I remember."

"Well, one thing you probably didn't know is she desperately wanted to let her sister know, to come visit us in her last days. But nobody was available to go. We had a couple of couriers who'd visit us from other towns from time to time—but no couriers based in Seabrook. And of course, our best friends all wanted to be there when she died, so they didn't go off to find my aunt."

He stared at the clouds, and his eyes moistened. "When she finally died, of course I was sad, but I also swore to myself not to let people suffer like that. I mean, people die all the time, but half of my mom's suffering was knowing she wouldn't talk to her sister ever again. I didn't really know about couriers at the time, but I met one a few months later, and it was less than a year after that I decided to become one myself."

He smiled and shrugged. "It was good to get out of town. Being in other places helped me think about other things."

"Makes sense to me."

"I've traveled all over the entire kingdom of Arendon, as far south as Valencia. I seem to spend a lot of time in Lugo."

"Have you ever seen the king?"

"Just from a distance. Feels like the general there runs things more than the king, though. He's the one who actually deals with the people, anyway."

They grew quiet and listened to the forest. A gentle breeze blew across their faces, and some nearby birds chattered to each other. The forest seemed peaceful, and

Amber enjoyed the feeling of connection she had with it whenever she was away from the village. Maybe that was part of why she wanted to leave?

She began to sing an old traveling song.

As I wander through the land,
Times of peace are here at hand,
Beauty small and beauty grand,
For my pleasure.
Birds are singing in the trees,
Lights are spinning by at ease,
Love and life are in the breeze,
Beyond measure.

Ryder smiled as she sang. Her voice was crisp and beautiful. The sun was bright enough to light the dirt road through the trees, and the two friends continued to appreciate the beauty around them as they rounded hill after hill toward the east. Finally, the road split, and they turned left toward lush green fields. As they rounded the next crest, they saw the old man's cottage sitting on a bright flower-covered hill by a creek.

"Hello, Mr. Thompson!" Amber called as they approached.

An old man stood in the doorway and waved at them. He wore a sharp-looking bright-red shirt, a black-brimmed hat, and a white beard that went down past his neck. A black dog came and sat next to him without a sound. As they grew nearer, Amber noticed the wrinkles on his face were deeper than the last time she'd visited. Had it really been that long?

He smiled an enormous, toothy grin. "Amber, my dear!" he exclaimed. "Why, you've grown so tall! You must be thirteen by now."

"Twelve," Amber said proudly.

"Indeed."

She dismounted, and they hugged each other. Then Mr. Thompson held her at arm's length and took a closer look at her. Her long brown hair casually fluttered in the wind as she smiled. The combination of her confidence and hunting clothes made her appear older than she was.

"What gives me the pleasure of seeing you on this beautiful spring day?" Mr. Thompson spoke with great energy, even though his body looked frail with age.

"Trouble," Amber said.

Ryder chimed in, "Big trouble."

"And we need your advice," Amber went on. "Bad things are happening, and nobody in our town knows what to do."

Mr. Thompson pursed his lips and nodded. "I see. Sounds important. Well then, let's talk."

For the first time in two days Amber felt like she was in the presence of someone who was going to have something helpful to say about their recent troubles. Finally, they could learn something useful!

Chapter 6

A Bit of History

"WELL," AMBER BEGAN, "a flying creature burned the Peabody's wheat fields two days ago, and we think there's more going on. Like there were five goblins that came and killed a cow, and the pixies have all left. They were attacked by imps. That sort of thing. It's all happening at once, and nobody knows why."

"Do tell. Do tell." Mr. Thompson gazed at them with a thoughtful expression and pursed lips, nodding and stroking his wispy white beard. He cocked his head and lifted his finger to speak. "Well then, come in. Let's have some lunch." He turned and gestured inside his home.

"But what about the fires?" Amber had expected something wise to come from the old man's mouth, and wondered about his lack of urgency.

"A good meal shared with friends is more pressing than the troubles of tomorrow." Mr. Thompson cackled happily and opened the door to show them inside.

"I can only stay for lunch," Ryder said. "I must be off to Lugo."

"Of course. Of course." The old man's knees popped and cracked as he walked up the steps and through the door with his dog close behind.

Amber marveled at the amazing design of the little cottage. For such a seemingly small home from the outside, the kitchen and dining room were large, grand and bright, suitable to feed twenty people, like the great hall back in Seabrook. It was as if Mr. Thompson, despite living all alone, was prepared for hosting large feasts.

Mr. Thompson saw Amber marveling at the exquisitely crafted stove and smiled. "A beautiful piece of work, isn't it?"

"Ah, yes." Amber awkwardly put her hands in her pockets, realizing she'd been staring. "Um . . . why do you have such a . . . um . . ."

"Big and fantastic kitchen?" Mr. Thompson grinned ear to ear.

"Yes. That."

"You'd be surprised how well a good kitchen gets used when you're prepared to use it." The old man winked.

"But you're not near anyone."

"No matter. If you know what you want, it will come to you. Now then, let's eat. I just happen to have enough stew ready for three."

As Amber and Ryder sat down at the long table and watched Mr. Thompson serve up three large bowls, they were surprised. There was indeed enough stew for exactly three hungry people. How on earth had he known to make that extra food?

"My, my. How time has flown!" The old man talked between slurps. "I remember when you were just a wee little one, and your dad took you out on a fishing boat, and you nearly drowned."

"Really?" Amber leaned forward. "I didn't know that. What happened?"

"Oh, your parents never told you that story?" He chuckled. "They're probably too embarrassed! See, your uncle caught a fish *so* big, all the people in the boat wanted to see it, and they all got on one side of the boat and tipped it right over! Ha!"

He laughed, pleased with himself. "It's a miracle you

survived—but your dad's friend Larry dove down and grabbed you, pulled you right out of the water and pushed the water out of your lungs. You were totally fine!" He grinned, flashing crooked teeth. "And your uncle didn't lose the fish!"

Amber and Ryder laughed along with Mr. Thompson. Ryder gazed at him admiringly. "You must have lots of great stories over the years."

"Oh yes. Of course. Of course." Mr. Thompson sat back and gestured intricately with his hands as he talked. "See, when I was a youngster, like right around your age, I lived quite a ways from here, and the next village over had a giant who decided he wanted to live nearby. Oh the trouble he caused! He was huge—the size of three or four full grown men. And the people of the village didn't know what to do. Because, see, he would come rolling into town and pick up a cow and take it home for lunch. Unfortunately, some men tried to stop it, and the giant killed them instantly."

"What could anyone do? The little town didn't have any great warriors or such. The bravest men considered attacking it again—but to what end? What's a farmer going to do to a giant? But then an old man, goodness, he was probably about as old as I am now. How time flies. That old man watched the giant carefully every time it came and noticed that it always went for the most-plump cows. And so the old man got an idea."

"He convinced the villagers to bring their biggest, most-delicious looking cows to this one spot, which happened to be in a valley, see. And then, when the giant came rolling into town, the old man said, 'Oh great giant, all our best cows are grazing down the valley!' So what does that giant do but go strolling right into the valley, into a trap! When he got to the right spot, the villagers caused an avalanche right above him and buried that giant, once and for all!"

"I'll never forget how happy we all were. My village too, because we figured we were next after he ate all the cows at that village. Ah, that's probably the best story I've got." The old man leaned forward and grew quiet. "Unless you like stories about dragons." He grinned slyly.

Ryder laughed. "Oh, Mr. Thompson. Of *course* you have a story about dragons. You can't leave us hanging like this. Tell us."

"Real dragons?" Amber pressed her palms into the table. "Do tell us. Please, Mr. Thompson."

"Oh, alright then." Mr. Thompson dabbed some bread into his stew and continued. "It was about thirty years ago. Hmm. Maybe more like forty. Well, let's say thirty-five. Anyway, there was a dragon—a big green dragon—who suddenly decided it needed to live right next to the main road between two cities."

"I actually saw it once but not up close, thankfully. I was in one of the cities, and it was flying in the distance. Anyway, the problem was that it was an important road. Lots of people wanted to travel on that road. But unfortunately the dragon seemed to like eating people. You know, some dragons tend to eat cows or sheep. But this one was pretty nasty. And so the trade and travel completely dried up between the towns."

"Well, one of the cities, Lugo, had an army, and so they decided they'd send out fifty of their bravest soldiers to take it on. That didn't go so well. Because, see, dragons have fire and scales that are hard to penetrate and big teeth and claws. The men didn't stand a chance."

"And so the King of Lugo made a decree that if any hero could kill the dragon, they would receive a full chest of gold. I can tell you, I heard of quite a few trying. And there was one great hero with a magic sword who I think got pretty close. But nope. None of them did it. And the situation seemed hopeless. That is, until some kids had an idea."

Mr. Thompson looked at Amber with a mischievous grin and continued. "Three kids decided it was time to take things into their own hands. It just so happened that the spot the dragon was calling home was not too far from a small river. And so those kids went upstream from the dragon and spent all day piling up rocks and branches. They were building a dam, just like a beaver would, except theirs wasn't to live in. Their dam was for diverting the water!"

"Sure enough. Those kids kept at it all the next day, and near the end of the second day, they'd built it up high enough that the water changed course! Poor fish. But the water went down the hill, right into the road. The whole area filled up and created a big lake. So, of course, the dragon flew away. And who knows where it went! It just left! Ha! Ha! Ha!"

Mr. Thompson's laugh was contagious, and Amber and Ryder found themselves laughing along with him.

"Can you believe it? All those heroes and that high-falutin king's reward couldn't fix anything, but those kids did it by moving some rocks! It was no problem to clear the dam and put the river back to the way it was, and the dragon never came back. Ha! Ha! Ha!"

Ryder and Amber laughed till they cried. Finally, Ryder stood. "I hate to leave, but I must get to the next town before the afternoon passes. Thank you for your hospitality."

"Be safe out there," Mr. Thompson said, walking him to his horse.

"I always do," Ryder said, then turned and gave Amber a hug. "I'll be passing through Wakefield in a couple of days.

I'll keep my eyes peeled for you in case you head that way. I have a knack for finding people." He gave a wink.

Amber felt warm inside knowing she was being looked after. Ryder mounted his horse and waved, then rode off at a gallop.

Back inside, Mr. Thompson began cleaning dishes. "So how is old Danny? Is he still trying to build that dock idea of his?

"Oh yes. He's actually made some good progress on it. Not that it's perfect, mind you, but the ships can unload fish a lot easier with the staggered levels."

"Wonderful! And Mr. Meyer? Is he still trying out new bun recipes every Sunday?"

"Yes. He had a great one just last month. He rolled the bun and swirled it in cinnamon and sugar. He called it a cinnamon bun."

"Ah, I'd like to try one of those." Mr. Thompson licked his lips. "He always did have the baker's thumb!"

The old man never seemed to stand still. As he talked, he'd move around the kitchen and clean things, knead bread, tidy up a little corner, or rearrange seemingly random items.

Eventually, they took the conversation outside to a meticulous garden full of early spring greens, which he picked. Then they continued the conversation inside, next to a small bookcase. Amber wondered what sorts of books he might have.

At one point, Mr. Thompson went to the fireplace and put a log on the fire. Amber looked outside, startled. It was nearly dark. The entire afternoon had passed by in the blink of an eye.

"It's dinner time!" He brushed his hands and walked into the kitchen.

Amber watched him in awe. Somehow, the old man had managed to keep her occupied and prepare a meal right under her nose! He handed her two plates, knives, and forks, which she set on the table. They sat down with fresh baked bread, sausage, and a salad from the greens they'd picked earlier. The black dog, which had been closely following his every move the entire day, went to the other side of the room and lay down.

He continued to ask about different people in Seabrook. He seemed more interested in how the people were managing regular life than the newest troubling events.

The evening might have continued on that way, but Amber shook her head and abruptly changed the conversation. "Mr. Thompson, I don't mean to be pushy, but I'd really like to know what you think about our situation in Seabrook. Do you have any idea what's going on? Was it really a phoenix that burned our fields? Why are the pixies leaving? And what could be causing the goblins to come back—and the imps?"

He sat silently for a moment. "I wonder if we need to rephrase the questions." He tidied up a few last things in the kitchen, then sat down next to Amber, taking her hands in his. "What sorts of creatures can start fires in fields and be seen flying off? It could be a dragon, a phoenix, or perhaps a person riding a flying creature. But what of it? The real question is, *why* did they do it?"

"How can we know that?"

"Before we get to that, let's see if we can come up with some ideas."

"Ok." She hesitated, expecting him to say something else. But he sat in silence looking at her expectantly, so she continued, "Maybe it's mad at us for some reason . . ."

"Good, good." He patted her hands. "Keep going."

"Ok. Well, it could be an evil creature, maybe a new one that we don't know about."

Mr. Thompson nodded.

She continued, gaining momentum, "Or maybe it *is* the good phoenix we know from before, but something has turned it against us. Maybe there's some sort of magic going on that made the phoenix think we're enemies."

Mr. Thompson nodded slowly, and her eyes widened. "That makes sense, doesn't it? We haven't done anything against it, and nobody has heard of any new creatures around. It's turned against us, hasn't it? And something to do with magic could explain the imps coming and attacking the pixies! I wonder why the goblins are around, though."

The old man pulled on his beard in thought. "Magic being involved is a strong possibility, there is no doubt. Also, there have been some odd things around here." He gestured in big sweeping motions. "I've noticed the animals around here more skittish than usual, as if they're upset about something that's invaded their territory. We haven't seen goblins in these parts for many decades now, but the way the animals are acting seems familiar to me, like from back in the troll wars before you were born."

"Trolls, a dragon, a phoenix." Amber shook her head. "Any of these are beyond what my village knows how to handle. What can we do about it? How do we stop creatures like that without magic?"

Mr. Thompson reached for his pipe and lit it. He went to the fireplace and put another log on, then sat in a comfortable chair nearby, beckoning Amber to join him in the one next to him. He blew a few perfectly crafted smoke rings that floated up to the ceiling as if enchanted. "I'm no magician myself," he said between puffs. "And, as a general rule, I don't like trying to fix something I know nothing about. Which means . . ." he paused dramatically, "you're in need of a magician."

She sat puzzled for a moment. "Who?"

"I do know of a good wizard in our neck of the woods. He goes by the name of Sage. He can often be found in Wakefield, less than a day's ride east of here. You're going to need help beyond what you'll find in these parts. I have a feeling this is much bigger than what any of us around here knows how to deal with."

Amber gritted her teeth. It was beginning to look like she'd be traveling alone through unknown forests full of goblins or even trolls while searching for some wizard or other.

Her heart pounded and her mind raced as she watched Mr. Thompson make her a bed by the fire.

This is more than I am ready for, she thought. I'm in way over my head. But what other option do I have?

She stared into the flames and thought of the big fire she'd helped put out just two days before. Time was pressing. Something had to be done, and this was the best idea so far.

She gripped the enchanted rock from Flurry for a moment. No need to use it yet, but it was always there if Sage had no answers and she needed to find the way to more insight.

She closed her eyes and thought of her home. Most of the people would be settling in for the night, but now some people would be staying up and keeping watch. Maybe even her sister. Times had changed—and not for the better. She needed to find Sage as quickly as possible. There was no time to lose.

Chapter 7

Danger in the Woods

AMBER AWOKE SOON AFTER THE SUN ROSE to the smell of freshly cooked eggs and bread. Seeing her stagger to her feet, Mr. Thompson called from the kitchen, "A good meal starts the day off right!" He handed her a plate of eggs and fresh-baked bread, which she wolfed down, then he walked her outside.

"I've packed some tasty biscuits for lunch." He handed her a warm, bulging red napkin that smelled delicious, then walked to Buttercup to look over her supplies. "Every adventurer must ensure they have the proper gear." He patted the golden horse. "You seem well prepared."

"But I'm not an adventurer," Amber said.

The old man's smile looked cryptic. "Oh really? We'll see about that."

She shrugged awkwardly and mounted her golden horse with its white flowing mane.

Mr. Thompson handed her the reins. "You'll be making lots of decisions out there. Your heart can usually give better advice than the person next to you. And if you don't have the answer to your question, consider changing your question."

He paused and looked her in the eyes. "One more thing. When you have time to think, never let fear guide your decisions. There are many great motivators—love, honor, respect. But fear isn't one of them." With that he patted her horse and waved goodbye as Amber set off on the full-day's journey to Wakefield.

It was a beautiful spring day. The dirt road to Wakefield passed through rolling hills, with forest getting dense in the distance. The journey would take her past two large mountains, but for now the path felt open and safe.

Hours later, when she was riding along quietly, lost in her thoughts, she suddenly realized something didn't seem quite right.

She strained but couldn't hear any birds or even grasshoppers. The entire forest had gone quiet. She slowed

Buttercup to a stop and listened carefully. The wind whistled through the leaves of the tall trees, but no other sound could be heard.

Since she didn't know why the forest was so quiet, she thought, Ok. Then let's change the question, like Mr. Thompson said. Instead of asking why the forest is so quiet, let's ask, what kinds of things make forests go quiet?

She considered it. Predators could scare birds to stop chirping. Like a hawk. Perhaps something startled them.

It could be me, of course. Hope it's not a troll.

She found herself walking the horse more slowly.

Am I really old enough to be out here on my own? A troll . . . what would I do if I saw a troll?

She couldn't imagine. Even the thought of it made her question whether she should be more prepared—if she should pull out her bow or something.

Why did I think I was ready to do this?

A few minutes passed by as Amber grew more and more nervous. Suddenly a stocky dark creature leaped out of the nearby bushes, yelling wildly and waving a scimitar.

Amber screamed, and Buttercup reared, then took off straight into the woods, galloping at full throttle. She held on tightly as they brushed past trees. Branches slapped and stung her face and body, but she ignored the pain. She lowered her face to protect herself, then felt a large branch slam into her side, knocking the wind out of her and sending her to the ground, gasping for breath.

When she regained her breath, she listened. Buttercup continued to gallop into the woods. Behind her, creatures crashed through the brush toward her. Her heart stuck in her throat, and she glanced around, spying a large log. She leaped to her feet and dove behind it, just as the creatures plunged into her sight.

She'd never seen real goblins before. They were slightly shorter than her—but three times heavier. Their skin was dark green, and their bulging noses were covered with warts. Their yellow teeth were sharp, dirty, and menacing; their tongues lolled about like a dog's.

Amber ducked down and held her breath as the two goblins ran past. She lay on the ground listening to them whack their way through bushes and branches and snarl like warthogs. As the sound faded off into the distance, she stayed on the ground behind the log, her heart pounding wildly.

After the panic had subsided, her mind raced. Goblins! Just as the townsfolk had said. What am I doing out here alone? Why couldn't Ryder have waited and traveled with me? He'd have known what to do. The once-friendly woods seemed strange and dangerous.

Her options were bleak. All her supplies were on her horse. Getting to Wakefield on foot would take many days. She stood and breathed deeply. She had her bow and arrows, hunting knife, flint and steel, the enchanted stone from Flurry, and the medallion from her mom around her neck.

She didn't want to follow the goblins, but she did want to find Buttercup and her food supply. Otherwise, it would be a long, hungry day and a cold, dark night. With a sigh, she stood and straightened the bow on her shoulder.

Following the horse tracks, she walked much slower than normal, ready for something else to pounce out at her any minute. At one point, she thought she heard something crack a branch nearby, so she pulled out her bow and an arrow to reassure herself but eventually slung it back over her shoulder when nothing appeared.

A few hours into her journey, her stomach started to gurgle. She frowned and thought of the food in her saddlebags so far away. She stood and listened for a moment, then made her way to a nearby creek, being careful to look behind her often so she could find the way back to the horse tracks.

By the creek, she looked for a deeper pool and found some fish. She pulled off her bow and peered into the water with an arrow at the ready, then released it into the pool. No fish. She noticed the arrow was about a foot higher up than she had thought it would be and realized the reflection of the water was tricking her.

She pulled out another arrow and stood above the pool again, watching vigilantly. When the next large fish swam into her line of sight, she aimed a foot lower and released. This time the arrow went straight through the fish. She smiled, reached in, and pulled out both arrows.

With her flint and steel, she made a small fire—using only dead wood so there would be less smoke to draw attention—and roasted the fish on a stick. Using her knife, she cut off pieces, licking her lips as she hurriedly ate the fish, then extinguished the fire and left.

She found Buttercup's trail again and picked up where she'd left off. Occasionally she saw goblin tracks next to the horse tracks and wondered if the goblins had already caught Buttercup.

Do goblins eat horses? Or maybe they want the supplies? Would a goblin keep a horse to ride it?

Amber wasn't sure what she'd find, and the more she wondered what lay ahead, the more she didn't want to keep going. But so far, finding Buttercup was the only real action she could think to take, so she kept on. Besides, hadn't Mr. Thompson just told her to not let fear guide her decisions?

After another hour, the tracks led to a wide pasture. She didn't want to be exposed out in the open in case the goblins were around, but it didn't seem like there was much choice. Amber stood at the edge of the clearing and observed her surroundings. Birds were chirping nearby, as if to say, *no troubles here.*

She took a deep breath, held her bow with a notched arrow, then carefully walked out into the field. She had taken only a few steps when she heard a whistle pierce through the silence. She whirled toward the sound—it had come from the trees, to her right. She couldn't see anything at first, then noticed a small figure in the trees waving. She glanced around at the rest of the trees, then walked toward the person, keeping her bow and arrow ready.

As she got nearer, a boy only a few inches taller than her dropped out of the tree. He had curly brown hair, sharp blue eyes, and brown-and-green clothing that blended with the forest behind him. A short sword hung from his left side, and a bow and some arrows rested on his back.

He put his fists on his hips. "I'd be careful if I were you. Two goblins went that way, only twenty minutes ago." He nodded toward the other side of the field.

"Oh!" Amber's eyes brightened and she followed his gaze for a moment. "Did you see my horse?"

The boy raised his eyebrows. "You seem awfully glad to know goblins went that way. I, for one, like to go the opposite way of goblins." He regarded her curiously. "Why is that?"

She put her hands in her pockets nervously. "The goblins scared off my horse a few hours ago. But I need her. She's got all my things, and she's my favorite horse. I don't know what else to do, so I'm tracking her down."

"Huh." The boy tapped the hilt of his sword for a moment. "Well, I'd be awfully careful following those goblins. You know, they have an amazing sense of smell—it's hard to sneak up on 'em. In fact, they usually do a better job of sneaking up on us!"

Amber looked him over. He appeared to have spent several days in the woods—and his sword looked well worn. "Well, what would *you* do?"

The boy grinned. "I'd follow it, of course!"

She smiled and put out her hand. "My name's Amber. What's your name?"

"Basil." He took her hand. "Where are you from?"

"I've traveled from Seabrook."

"That's quite a ways." Basil gazed into space as if to calculate the exact distance. "What are you doing out here all by yourself?"

"I'm on a mission," she said proudly.

Basil cocked his head. "What sort of . . . mission?"

"A flying creature came and burned one of our fields. They think it was a phoenix. I'm going to find a wizard in Wakefield who can give us advice."

He stood quietly for a moment. "We've been having issues in my village as well, over there in Sanford." He pointed to the east. "A few weeks ago, we started seeing some random goblins—first time in decades. And now, it's like they're everywhere. Somebody even said they saw a troll. Something's changed, and nobody knows what."

"How far is your village?"

"Pretty close, actually. Only a few miles at this point. You're quite off track to head to Wakefield. That's about twenty miles that way." He pointed to their south.

"I have to find my horse first."

"Ok. Ok." Basil folded his arms. "Here's what I'm thinking. I want to find out what's going on too, and you definitely would be safer traveling with someone. I want to go with you. Let's see if we can get your horse back, and then go to my village for some supplies and talk to my parents."

Amber felt a bit lighter in spirit. Although she'd just met Basil, being with him seemed to instantly make the task easier.

Basil held out his hand. "Is it a deal?"

"It's a deal." They shook hands and headed toward the field. Now they just had to figure out how to sneak up on a couple of cranky goblins.

Chapter 8

New Friends

THE GOBLINS SAT BY A FIRE, smacking their mouths loudly. Buttercup stood tethered to a tree twenty feet away, looking uneasy and ready to bolt. From a closer distance, the goblins' hideous appearance was more obvious. They had dark green skin full of blemishes and warts, scrawny black hair—matted and running down their backs—and enormous bellies. They wore battered, poor-quality leather armor and sturdy-looking boots. Their sharp teeth tore into the mutton Amber's mom had prepared so caringly, causing pieces of food and drool to fall onto their bodies.

"That's *my* food!" Amber whispered to Basil.

"What did you expect?" he whispered back.

Thankfully, the goblins were making so much noise, and with their mouths full, it was pretty obvious they wouldn't be smelling or hearing anything. Amber and Basil crouched behind a bush, bows in their hands.

"If they attack, let's shoot at the same time," he whispered.

"Ok." Her eyes darted around nervously.

Basil pointed to their right. "We need to sneak around this way and steal the horse back. Let's be ready with our arrows."

Amber stood to draw an arrow, causing a branch to crack under her foot. The nearest goblin snapped its head up and looked straight into her eyes. She instantly felt the evil behind its gaze and knew it intended to kill her. The goblin leaped to its feet, drew a rusted scimitar, and dashed toward them faster than either of them expected.

They let their arrows fly and hit the goblin in the chest—perfect shots! The goblin fell to the ground and yelled, "Raaah!"

It scrambled to its feet and staggered toward them again, waving the curved sword. The second goblin was now right behind it with a knobby club.

Amber and Basil drew arrows again and let them fly.

"Aaaaaaah!" the goblin yelled, raising its scimitar above its head, now with four arrows protruding from its chest.

Amber drew another arrow as Basil dropped his bow and drew his short sword. The blade rang as it left its scabbard.

She let the arrow fly, right before the goblin was on them, and it hit the goblin in the throat. The goblin stumbled to the ground face-first in front of them. Her heart was beating so loudly, she couldn't hear anything else.

The second goblin came quickly. Before Amber could draw another arrow, Basil attacked it with his sword.

The goblin blocked, and the sound of clanging metal filled the woods. Basil turned and thrust the sword toward the goblin, piercing its chest, a few inches deep.

It let out a yell and swung wildly, off-balance. Amber saw her moment and let loose another arrow. The goblin staggered to the side, and Basil quickly thrust again, finishing it off. The creature slumped to the ground, wide-eyed, and landed facedown in front of Amber.

She stood, shaking and breathing heavily, then stepped back, drew another arrow, and watched the goblins' bodies carefully. Basil nudged each goblin with his foot, sword at the ready. When neither responded, the young warriors let out a breath of relief.

Amber ran to her horse and hugged its neck. "Are you ok, Buttercup? Did those nasty goblins hurt you?" She examined the horse's body. All seemed fine, and the remaining supplies were mostly intact.

Basil had an air of bravado in his voice. "I knew we could do it. Simple. Only two goblins after all." He wiped his blade and sheathed it in the scabbard on his side.

She looked at him incredulously. He'd handled his sword well, but she guessed it had been his first encounter with goblins, just like her. Still, she was happy to have him there. It would have been close to impossible for her to take on goblins on her own—nothing like hunting.

Basil bent over the goblins, looking at something, then said, "It's getting late."

As if on cue, a chilly breeze pierced through their clothing. "Let's ride back to Sanford. If we hurry, we'll get there before dark."

She mounted her horse, and then gave a hand to Basil, who climbed up behind her. With a kick of her heels, they were off, galloping at a steady pace.

"What were you looking at—on the goblins?" she called back over her shoulder.

"I wanted to see what they were carrying."

"Oh? Was there anything interesting?"

"Well, first off, there were three silver pieces and some copper."

Amber's eyes lit up as she rode. She hadn't thought the goblins would have money. Three silver pieces could be very helpful. "And was there something else?"

"Yes, there was a small pendant on a chain with a design on it. I'm going to show it to some folks in town."

"Sounds like a good idea!" she called back over her shoulder. They would know more soon, she hoped.

They saw the lights of the village as dusk approached. Amber sighed with relief as they entered through the large wooden gate, the forest far behind them.

Basil pointed. "This way."

Amber had only been to other small towns like hers, along the coast. The street they walked down was wider and smoother than back in Seabrook. A few people looked curiously at them as they passed. They made their way down a few winding streets till they arrived at a small house. She tied Buttercup to a post, and they walked inside.

A woman's voice called, "Make sure you take your muddy boots off!"

Basil grinned at Amber and removed his boots after hanging up his cloak. "Hi, Mom! I've got someone to introduce you to."

A brownish-blonde woman with friendly wrinkles around her eyes walked into the main room, holding a towel.

"This is Amber." Basil patted her on the shoulder. "I met her in the woods. She's from Seabrook."

"Well, that's quite the distance." Basil's mother raised her eyebrows. "What brings you out here? Don't you know there've been lots of goblin sightings in these parts?"

"Yes, ma'am." Amber nodded. "I didn't expect to come this way. I was heading to Wakefield when goblins attacked. Basil helped me get my horse back."

"Oh dear. Are you ok?" She looked Amber over, then Basil.

"Yes. We shot the first one five times." Basil's eyes lit up, and he gestured grandly. "And I killed the second with my sword." He patted the hilt of his sword proudly. "Also, I found this." He pulled the pendant out of a pocket. "There's an interesting design on it."

"Oh, Basil. I told you to be careful out there! Everyone is saying the goblins are all over the place! I'm so thankful you found each other." She had a worried look on her face.

"Of course, Mom." Basil lifted his head and put his fists on his hips. "It was easy. We did it without a scratch. Here. Take a look." He held the pendant out to her.

She inspected it. "We should show this to Chandler."

"Yep. I was thinking the same thing."

"Well. You must be hungry. It's very late, and I imagine you haven't had a good meal all day."

Basil grinned. "You got that right!"

Amber was used to simple food like bread and vegetables, sometimes seafood, and meats only on special occasions. Basil's family ate potatoes and chicken with spices that at first seemed unusual, then enticing.

She was struck by how Basil seemed to be the most animated of the family. He had four younger siblings who ate quietly and listened to him tell the story of how they'd killed the goblins with great gusto—and with more detail than Amber had remembered.

He embellished the story, making the goblins sound bigger and even nastier than they were. Amber might have corrected her own brothers, but she was so tired she was happy to let Basil continue. She noticed his dad, seated at the head of the table, nodding approvingly. He looked wise and thoughtful, with the same curly hair as Basil.

". . . and then, with four arrows stuck out of its massive chest, Amber sent a fifth arrow straight into its neck!" Basil made a gesture like an arrow flying through the air and acted like the goblin, falling back in his chair. The other children laughed and applauded, and Amber smiled.

She leaned back when she finished her plate. She hadn't realized how hungry she'd been. Encountering and killing the goblins had exhausted her physically and emotionally. She yawned.

Basil's mother instantly turned to her. "I suppose we'd better set you up with a bed. We've got some mats we can roll out by the fire."

"That would be lovely." Amber stretched and stood. "I have bedding with Buttercup. Oh! Buttercup! I need to take care of her."

"Don't worry, I can do it." Basil stood. "She can spend the night with Storm."

Amber raised her eyebrows and walked outside with Basil. They led her horse to a small stable with a single, beautiful black horse that stood quietly in a spacious stall.

Storm perked up when he saw Basil, flicking his ears and prancing about. Basil patted his neck. "Hi, Storm. You have a visitor."

Amber led Buttercup next to Storm and watched as the two horses observed each other. When they seemed fine with one another, Basil helped Amber take off Buttercup's saddle and saddlebags, then put them on the railing.

"Get your rest, and tomorrow we'll see about finding this wizard of yours. But first, I want to show the goblin's pendant to Chandler. It's different from the others we've seen around here."

Amber nodded and followed Basil, tired to her bones. As she prepared her bed, she thought of her friends and family back home, wondering if they were ok and what would happen to them if the phoenix returned.

Her mind continued to wander. This wizard, Sage, what if he can't save us from all these problems? It seems like it's far worse than just attacks on my village. Something bigger is going on. What can one wizard—or any of us—do about it?

She realized she was clenching her jaw and released it. However much she wanted to solve the problems of her village, she also needed her sleep, so she tried her hardest to relax, even if just for a moment.

Chapter 9

Pursuit of Pixies

A MAN WEARING ALL BLACK rode on a flapping hippogriff along the coast, scanning the craggy rocks and tall trees beyond the pebble beaches. The body of the hippogriff was like a sturdy dark-brown horse, and it had the front legs and head of a massive golden eagle. It glistened in the afternoon sun as it slowly beat its gigantic wings, obediently following the man's silent direction.

He scowled. His leather armor and cape matched his mood, as dark as the night. He had a sizable black beard, a thin short sword on his left side, and a silver scepter in a holster of sorts on his right. Even darker than his appearance was the spirit emanating from him, an evilness that scattered seagulls in every direction as he approached.

He pulled a thin wooden wand out of his belt and pointed it toward the coast. "Illuminado!" His voice was full of power and he held the wand steady.

He frowned deeply and continued scanning the rugged old trees along the rocky coast. The trees rustled in the wind as the waves crashed along the pebbles and larger rocks. Nothing out of the ordinary was visible.

He slowed down as another hippogriff approached from the coastline, bearing a rider wearing dark clothing and a long red cape that fluttered in the wind.

The other rider turned his steed to fly in the same direction alongside the first one. "I've found them, Lucio!" He was much younger looking and brown-skinned, with a neatly trimmed, very short black beard. He looked quite friendly compared to the menacing dark man.

"Where?" Lucio asked.

"Five miles up the coast. They're heading west, as we anticipated."

"Excellent. Show me."

The two lifted higher into the air and flew along the shoreline. They passed a village where people were tending a field that had recently been burned by a large fire. There was a shout from the village far below, but the men ignored it as they flew steadily west.

"How many?" Lucio called.

"At least a few dozen," the other man called back over the wind. "It's hard to say. The imps have killed at least one or two. But not more than that."

They flew in silence, then the younger man said, "They're down here. In the thick trees."

The dark man nodded, and they glided down to some rocks on the shoreline. The hippogriffs landed gracefully and folded their wings so the men could dismount. Both men were light on their feet, agile like cats, and disembarked with barely a sound. They strode to the tree line, next to the coast, and paused.

Lucio folded his arms and stood peering into the woods, then pulled his wand from his belt and raised it. "*Illuminado!*" The words came out quietly but forcefully.

He smiled, a wicked grin. "They are here, as you say. We will kill most of them—but not all. We need to leave a few of them, so they can lead us to their Great Stone Tower."

He turned to the younger man who was nodding. "Yes. Yes, of course. What's your plan? Magic?"

"Pixies have a way of countering spells, as you should know, Caster," Lucio said calmly. "But yes, magic will work well for us in this case." He put the wand back in his belt, then pulled the silver scepter off his side. He turned to the trees around him and waved the scepter. The tip glowed purple briefly, then a dozen birds came flying out of the trees toward him.

They hovered in front of him as he spoke. "Go to the pixies and report back to us where they are at all times. If they move, let us know immediately."

The birds scattered in different directions, and Lucio holstered the scepter. "Let's give them a couple of minutes. We need to be certain. Any imps left?"

"Just one. Would you like me to call it?"

"Yes."

Caster lifted a small brown wand and spoke quietly but with force, "Reconicio." They waited for a minute, then the imp flew out from the trees to their right and hovered in front of them.

Lucio spoke. "Ask it what it knows."

Caster lifted his wand peered at the imp, as if searching its soul. After a moment he said, "They've killed the other imps. They are as treacherous as ever. There are pixies from two villages in the group. Roughly fifty or so. They seem to have purpose in their direction, not wandering around. They're definitely heading somewhere."

"Has the imp been noticed?" Lucio asked. "Ask it. Even if it thinks it's minutely possible."

Caster focused again. "Most likely not. It's uncertain, but it hasn't killed any pixies, so it thinks they don't know about it yet. It also says the pixies are edgy, watching the woods with great intensity. The chance of sneaking up on them is slim, and that's for an imp."

He stroked his short black beard, then looked at Lucio with raised eyebrows. "I assume you have a plan?"

"Of course." Lucio put the scepter back in its holster. "We'll know when it's time to attack. The key to taking on pixies is to use their own powers against them. They trust the forest—so we will turn the forest into a prison."

The first of the birds returned, and Lucio held the scepter up again, listening, as the tip glowed purple. "They're this way. Come on then."

They quietly walked through the woods, careful not to step on any branches or leaves. Lucio gestured with his hands, making a motion that signaled Caster to walk to his right side. They slowly walked up to a thicket, then circled around on either side.

There, they could hear dozens of pixies chatting and fluttering in the wind, their tiny voices lifting high above the other forest sounds.

Lucio gestured, and counted down on his fingers. Three. Two. One.

He raised his wand and urgently whispered, "Ballistico!"

The branches above the clearing suddenly shifted and turned into arrows of sorts, raining down on the entire area.

Caster waved his wand around the area. "Protexin!"

A translucent, shimmering wall surrounded the grove of trees. Some of the arrows bounced off branches and flew toward the semi-invisible wall but ricocheted off toward the forest floor.

As hundreds of arrows flew down, covering the area over and over, the sound of cracking and rushing wind filled the once-peaceful forest. Plants with wide leaves were ripped apart, and a few mushrooms exploded into flying pieces.

When the sound died down, Lucio gave a signal, and Caster snapped his fingers, causing the glowing wall to disappear. The two men walked into the devastated area and looked around.

Lucio frowned. "Where are they?"

Caster silently shrugged and looked underneath a bush.

Lucio slapped a small tree with his wand. "How did they escape?"

He peered into a bush, then scrutinized a larger tree looking for cracks. "They were here!"

"Are you sure?" Caster asked. "We heard them, but did you see them?"

Lucio paused. "Do you think they knew we were coming? Do you think they cast a spell to trick us?"

Caster shrugged and looked a bit sheepish. "Yeah, I do. They're tricky little buggers. They probably figured out the birds were enchanted, or maybe they were watching the imp. Who knows? But they're obviously not here, and they fooled us into thinking they were."

Lucio raised his wand. "Illuminado!"

They stood in silence, listening to the forest return to its prior state with birds chirping and squirrels scrambling from branch to branch.

"Argh!" He kicked a branch, sending it flying into a tree, then stormed through the woods back toward the coast. Caster looked around one last time and followed quickly behind. As Lucio went, he muttered to himself, whacking the occasional leafy bush with his wand and causing it to wilt.

They emerged back into the sun on the rocky coastline, the great glistening sea before them, white caps breaking the waves in the wind. Lucio turned to Caster. "They may have fooled us this time, but we're on their trail. We'll continue to burn the villages along the coast. More pixies will emerge. But we'll need more imps."

He paused and glared.

Caster gulped loudly. "I . . . um . . . I know who to ask where we might find more. I think most of them in this area are long gone."

"Good." Lucio folded his arms and stared at the waves. "We'll need them. I don't care if you have to cross the sea. They're important to our plan. They're the most effective way to track the pixies."

As if on cue, the imp flew over to Caster. "And this one?"

"Tell it to keep a low profile. We can't let it get killed— yet. We need it to pick up the trail of the pixies again. But tell it to keep its distance. We don't really need to kill the pixies right now. We need at least some of them to make it to their tower."

Caster raised his wand and looked into the imp's eyes. After a moment, it flew off into the forest, and Caster turned back to Lucio. "So . . . is that all you need from me here? Shall I find more imps?"

Lucio nodded. "Yes. Get moving at once. And I'll check on the army. Let's reconvene in a few days at the queen's fortress."

Caster bobbed his head. "You got it. I'll see you there."

Both men mounted their hippogriffs, then kicked their sides. The creatures spread their enormous wings and gracefully lifted into the sky. Caster flew southwest, and Lucio flew due south.

As the flying figures vanished, dozens of small pixie heads popped out of hidden pockets in nearby trees. They were smiling and patting each other on the backs. Although they were glad that they'd escaped the attack, their dilemma was now clear.

Evil wizards were after them for some reason. They were powerful, dangerous, and seemed to have a lot more help that hadn't been used yet. Something would have to be done, or they'd eventually be tracked down and killed.

Flurry shook her head. "Oh Amber. I hope you figure something out soon."

Chapter 10

A Better Plan

AMBER AWOKE WITH A START. The sun had been up for hours already, and it wasn't like her to sleep in so late. She looked around the room, getting her bearings. It took her a moment to remember that she was in another village, in another house.

Then she thought of her parents. Would they be worried if she didn't get word to them? She'd have to figure that out. She rolled up her bedding and looked around.

No one was inside the tidy house. Some sliced bread and cheese sat on the counter. She helped herself to some, then walked outside.

The sun shone, and she noticed for the first time the orange and purple daylilies surrounding Basil's house. She wandered into the street and took in the buildings around her. Some looked much like the ones in Seabrook, but there was something different about many of them. The buildings were more tightly packed together and taller, but there was something else she couldn't put her finger on.

Amber peered at a house, trying to figure out what the difference was, then it struck her: the windows. In Seabrook, all the windows had shutters for big storms, and the windows themselves were divided into four or more. But here, the windows were large, empty, and sparse in comparison.

Sanford was also much bigger than Seabrook. She couldn't tell how large it was but there seemed to be a lot more people around.

After wandering for a few minutes, Amber realized she might get lost if she didn't find a landmark. She looked back and noted a large, grey rock next to a blue house by the dirt road, then turned and kept walking.

She came across two men dressed in elegant white shirts with fancy collars and jackets with intricate patterns. "Good morning." Amber waved. "Do you by any chance know where Basil might have gone off to?"

One of the men smiled. "Who's Basil?"

She was taken aback. In her town, everybody knew everybody. It never struck her before that a town could be large enough that someone may not know someone else.

"Do you know where Chandler is?"

The man nodded. "Of course." He pointed down the road where she was headed. "If you stay on this road and turn right at the green house just over there, it's about ten houses down on the right. Two-story yellow building."

"Thank you." Amber gave a polite nod and then continued on her way, marveling at the houses. There were only three two-story houses in Seabrook, whereas this place had two-story houses everywhere. Basil's neighborhood was all homes, but now the buildings were mostly shops of different sorts, with living space on the second floors.

Every store had a sign hanging from it above the door with pictures of what they offered. She tried to guess what they were as she walked past them. Barbershop. Bar. Clothing store. Grocery store. Something to do with books.

Amber was so busy looking at the buildings that she walked into a bush with small leaves. "Oops!" she said out loud to no one in particular.

The bush was different than any she'd seen before, with tiny white berries and twisty branches that held her in. She tried not to damage the branches as she pulled herself out.

There was something comforting about the bush, and she wondered if it had helpful properties like healing. As she usually did with new plants, she made a mental note to look into it later.

She ended up in front of a two-story yellow building with a sign that looked like something to do with maps. Inside, maps and books lined every wall. Two large tables were in the main room, covered with open maps and a few books. At the back was a smaller table with a lamp, and Basil was there holding out the goblins' pendant to a middle-aged man with glasses.

Basil looked up and waved her over. "Amber. Come on in! This is Chandler."

Chandler wore nice clothing, with a collared shirt and billowy sleeves—the kind of clothing the people of Seabrook reserved for a wedding or special occasion. Amber watched curiously how he examined the pendant. He took off his glasses and put a big lens in his right eye to peer at it more closely.

"Hmm. Hmm." He frowned and pursed his lips as he turned it over and over. Finally he set it down and put his glasses back on.

"Well. The best guess I have is that there are different groups of them." He held up another pendant, very similar to the one Basil had taken off the goblin, but with a different design.

"These ones seem to be the most common in our parts. I think the goblins with these are coming from the mountains far to the south of here, the Ancares Mountains." Chandler pointed at the map on the table in front of them. "The one you found is a mystery . . . we haven't seen it yet. I wonder if it came from the west, over here." He pointed at another section of the map.

Amber had seen maps before, but this map had an amazing amount of detail and covered a much larger area. She saw Seabrook on the coast, far north of Sanford, and mentally thought of how far the towns were from each other. A full day's travel.

She looked at Wakefield, about the same distance away from Sanford. The Ancares Mountains, she figured, were well over two hundred miles away to the southeast.

The door opened, and Basil called, "Theo! Come here."

A skinny boy about Basil and Amber's age walked in. He wore fancy clothing that seemed suited more for city life than the outdoors. His shirt was a brilliant white with intricate designs and big sleeves, much too loose for things like archery, sword fighting, or climbing trees. He walked over to the table and immediately introduced himself to Amber.

"Hi. I'm Theo." He had straight blond hair, a few freckles, and a large grin. He put his hand out.

She smiled back. "I'm Amber." She took his hand.

"You must live in a tree?" Theo pointed at her clothes.

Amber raised her eyebrows, puzzled, then looked down at herself. She was covered in tiny leaves that looked as if they were glued to her clothing. "That's odd." She pulled one off. They were the leaves from the bush she'd walked into earlier. Then as if they'd been held on magnetically, they all dropped to the floor.

"Cool trick!" Theo grinned. "You'll have to show me sometime. Watch this one." He took a coin from his pocket and held it in one hand, then made it disappear in front of her eyes. She stared wide-eyed, looking at his empty hand.

"Magic." Theo winked. "Look at this—it ended up behind your ear." He reached behind her ear and revealed the coin. Amber's mouth opened, and Theo grinned. "I guess they don't do magic tricks in your tree, do they?"

She was about to say something when Basil interrupted. "Hey, Butterballs. Look at this." Basil held out the goblin pendant.

Theo took the pendant from Basil and held it up. "It's different from the other ones. What's your theory?" As he spoke, a white-and-black splotchy kitten came dashing from

the back and crawled up his leg. It perched on his shoulder and nestled its head into his neck. Without looking, he patted the kitten with one hand while holding the pendant up with the other.

Chandler pointed at the map. "I'm thinking it might have come from these mountains to the south. It would have to be underground, from what we know about goblins, so a place with caves. Look here."

He opened a book that had been sitting on the table and leafed to a page partway through. Under the heading *Dwellings*, there was a drawing of a goblin that looked much like the one Amber and Basil had encountered.

"It says here that goblins tend to live in mountainous or other cave areas, staying mostly underground until they have a good reason to leave. Which means—"

"They must have a good reason to leave, not just from one location, but from multiples." Theo said matter of factly. He put the pendant back on the table and grabbed the kitten off his shoulder, petting it in his arms. It began to purr loudly.

Chandler nodded. "Exactly. So our first idea that something happened in the Ancares Mountains is probably not exactly right. There is something much bigger going on here that has caused goblins to come out from far across the land."

"That's not all," Amber chimed in. Everyone turned to look at her. "We had a phoenix, or some other flying creature, come and burn a field in Seabrook."

"Interesting." Chandler stood and went to a shelf to get a piece of tracing paper. He placed the paper over the map and quickly traced the coastline, then added dots for a few of the villages and towns.

He drew a mountain in the middle of the Ancares mountain range and a cave opening. He put an "X" over the mountain, the cave, and Seabrook. Then he connected them, forming a triangle.

"We are here," he pointed with his pencil, "in the middle of these three events. The question is, are they occurring further out, or do we happen to live in the epicenter of the activity? In other words, is something nearby causing all of this to happen—or is it happening farther away as well?"

Amber thought for a moment. Chandler was an interesting man. He'd never introduced himself . . . he was too involved in his books and maps and ideas. He definitely made her think, although in this case, she didn't have any idea how to answer his question.

But then she remembered Mr. Thompson's advice to reframe the question. "Whether we're in the center or not, something has caused the creatures to come out. So the real question is, what could it be?"

Chandler turned to Amber and cocked his head. "Excellent question. Excellent indeed." He sat with a cocked head and raised finger, then abruptly stood and went to a far bookshelf, looking through the labels.

"Let's see . . . it's got to be here somewhere."

He paused at one book, took it off the shelf, and leafed through the pages. "No, not that one . . ."

He put it back and continued looking across the book spines. "This one!"

He smiled as he carried a large, old book with split leather binding and faint gold lettering over to the table where the three were waiting.

The title of the book was *History of the Upper Lands in the Age of Erlich.*

Amber pursed her mouth. She wouldn't have thought to open a history book for answers. In fact, she realized this entire process of discovery was far different than anything she'd experienced in her little home village. The people there were focused on action and practical steps. These people were treating the problems like a riddle to be solved through books, maps, and a history lesson.

Chandler tenderly flipped through many pages, then exclaimed, "Eureka! Here. Look!" He pointed at a page halfway down. "This happened nearly two hundred years ago, same exact thing. You see, all the villages and cities were bombarded by creatures, mostly evil ones like goblins but also good ones, like the phoenix. In those days, it was more common to see things like goblins and trolls in normal life. Not like today, where they've been gone a long time."

"Unfortunately, a few major cities and many villages were taken over, and the people who survived fled to other cities. Turns out, part of the reason the goblins were so successful was because they were being controlled by a powerful spell."

"Controlled is perhaps the wrong word," he said, looking up. "From what I can gather, it's like they were spurred in a certain direction." He looked back at the book. "There was a huge battle on the plains of Almeda. There were dragons, giants, trolls, ogres, and goblins, lots of goblins. While the people battled, there was another battle raging as well."

Chandler looked up and adjusted his glasses. "A battle of the wizards! Wizards on each side. The good wizards won the day, and the spell was lifted. With the spell gone, the creatures dispersed, each to their own homes, no longer intent on working together. You see, at their core, these creatures are all selfish and wouldn't work together without someone to guide them."

Chandler paused a moment and looked thoughtfully around the room. "Wizards. Magic. Spells. There's only one surefire way to figure out if the goblins are coming out because of magic. We need to find a wizard."

Amber cleared her throat. "Actually, I was on my way to finding a wizard when we were attacked by those goblins."

"Oh?" Chandler asked. "Where were you going?" He looked at her as if seeing her for the first time. Amber wondered how he still hadn't asked her name. It was as if he had no interest in her, only in the way she could help him solve the challenge.

"Wakefield," Amber replied.

"Ah, not far at all," Chandler mused. "We might even make it today if we were to leave now." He looked around. "Wouldn't need to pack very much. We could be home tomorrow."

Amber was taken aback. She looked at Basil, who had a look of excitement and eagerness on his face.

"Not me," said Theo haltingly. "It's my turn to take care of the goats this evening."

"Come on!" Basil punched his arm playfully. "You never leave town. Can't you come on this one little trip?"

Theo frowned at Basil, then glanced at Amber. He

looked nervous just thinking about it.

Amber gave a meek smile. "Your company would be welcome, and I'd like you to show me more of your tricks."

Theo hesitated. "Well . . . let me see if I can get out of my chores." He didn't seem excited like Basil but smiled back at Amber.

"Ok then, it's settled." Chandler stood, knocking a book onto the floor. "We'll leave at once!"

Chapter 11

Search for a Wizard

THE GOBLINS HAD EATEN some of Amber's food, but her provisions were mostly still intact from when she'd left her home a few days earlier. Sadly, Mr. Thompson's biscuits were gone, but Basil's mother had graciously given her some more food to pack, including dried meat and fruit, which she took thankfully.

As she was checking over Buttercup, yelling came from inside Basil's house. It sounded like a shouting match between Basil and his father. Amber tried not to listen in but heard Basil shout, "You're such a control freak! I'm glad I'm leaving!"

He blustered outside in a fury and slammed the door behind him. Amber focused on Buttercup's straps, adjusting and readjusting them awkwardly as Basil stormed over.

He huffed about, slamming some rope into a saddlebag. After gathering a few more items and looking Storm over, his breathing slowed.

Amber kept her eyes on her horse's straps. "You don't want to leave like that. What if you never make it back? My dad always says to make sure the last thing you say to someone isn't something you'd regret—just in case."

"Whatever," Basil said, mounting his horse. He kicked it in the sides, and it galloped onto the dirt road.

Amber jumped onto Buttercup, then quickly followed behind until she caught up with Basil. She rode next to him and looked at his face. His jaw was clenched, he had a fire in his eyes, and he tried not to look back at her.

He finally glanced over and sighed. "I'll be right back."

He turned his horse around, galloped back to the house, and ran inside. Several minutes later, he emerged and rode next to Amber again, as they headed toward Theo's house.

They rode in silence for a few minutes, then Basil turned to her with a sheepish smile. "Thanks."

He quickly looked back to the road and scratched his head awkwardly, ruffling his dark curls.

Amber sighed in relief. Soon they rounded up to Theo's house where he was outside with his parents, packing a warm coat into the saddlebags of his already overly burdened splotchy horse, Butterfly. A few hugs later, the three trotted down the street to Chandler's house.

Chandler had accurately calculated that Wakefield was less than a day's journey away—but grossly underestimated how much time it would take him to get ready. Amber and Basil were ready to go at barely a moment's notice. Even Theo, who rarely left town and had no proper clothing or supplies, was ready within an hour.

Meanwhile, Chandler had to pore over his books and maps, deciding which ones were important enough to bring and which should be left behind. He packed far too many at first—fifty-three books and eight maps—and he had to go through them all one by one, setting aside the less critical ones. In the end, he still brought eight books and three maps, but at least they fit in his saddlebags.

The road leading to Wakefield was hard packed and well-traveled and felt safer than any of the other roads Amber had taken so far. Maybe it helped that she now had three traveling companions, and there were other people traveling on the road in both directions.

She felt content as they rode along together, the sun on

her face. Theo was saying something that caused Basil to laugh, and although she couldn't hear anything in particular, she smiled with them as she rode next to Chandler, listening to him tell her a history lesson about the wizard war from two hundred years before.

The road wound through the mountains with forests sometimes right next to them for the first few miles, much like Amber was used to. But then it opened into a vast space with fields, rolling hills, and occasional trees, where she felt like she could see forever when they reached the top of one of the hills. At one point, she saw the city in the distance, then realized they were still many miles and a couple of hours away.

Chandler, it turned out, was an eccentric teacher of sorts, and Basil and Theo were two of his primary students. He knew much about the world and was eager to share his knowledge with Amber. But he had an awkward way of holding himself, like he was never truly comfortable sitting still. And he never once looked her in the eyes, which she found distracting at first but then got used to it and simply listened to him as she gazed at the countryside.

She hadn't had much schooling, although she did know how to read and write, unlike many from her village. And she read as many books as she could get her hands on, especially ones with adventure. But her small village didn't have many books, and most of the people were focused on survival: fishing, farming, hunting, and maintaining their village through difficulties. Chandler's seemingly endless knowledge was exciting to her, and she lapped it up like a thirsty dog.

It seemed like no time at all before they arrived at Wakefield. If Sanford was large compared to Seabrook, Wakefield was that much larger. The main road became cobblestone as they got nearer, and Amber realized how important that must be with so many wagons and horses traveling it, especially when the weather got wetter. They entered the main gate and began looking for a likely place to ask about the wizard Sage.

Amber was taken aback by the sheer number of people. They were everywhere—walking around, standing and talking to each other, hauling loads on wagons behind horses.

She tried to understand it all: Where are they all going? What do they do inside a town all day? How much time do they spend outside the walls of the town?

It wasn't just the size and busyness that startled her but also the unpleasant smells. She was shocked at how people left their garbage outside in barrels on the street, stinking up the entire town. Not to mention the horse and donkey manure that covered the streets. The filth attacked her senses and overwhelmed her ability to focus on the task at hand.

There were no big signs that said *Wizards Here,* and she began to wonder what the plan was. But Chandler seemed confident of his direction, turning right at the next street and never stopping his educational session with her.

"Now you see . . ."—he pointed at a large barn to their left—"this was the first stop for many of the trading parties, before they built the larger stable on the outskirts of town."

She nodded and kept listening. Chandler knew so much history about this one town, she wondered how much he might know about hers—or any other town for that matter.

"Ah, here we are." Chandler clapped his hands.

They came to a two-story building with a sign much like the one on his own, with a map etched onto the surface. The travelers dismounted and stretched. It was getting late. A man with a long pole tipped with fire lit the streetlamps. There were lampposts every fifty yards or so, all the way down the street.

The inside of the building was a larger version of Chandler's place in Sanford. People sat at tables, reading or discussing things quietly. Chandler walked up to one of them, a mid-aged, well-dressed man who was reading a large scroll at a table by himself.

"Ebeneezer, you old dog. How are you?" Chandler patted him on the back.

The man looked up and grinned. "Chandler! Well, well." He stood up, and the two men shook hands. "How'd your old cat handle that kitten?"

Chandler laughed. "Poorly. At first, she fought for her place, but the kitten overtook the rest of the house and kept trying to play with her, so she eventually found a little spot and just stayed there. But the kitten is happy, and the mice have definitely disappeared."

"Excellent!" Ebeneezer stood. He had a large belly and wore a jacket with ornate designs embroidered on the sleeves and pockets. He put his hands into his pockets and continued. "And your map of the five mountains? How's that coming along?"

"Good. Good." Chandler looked outside toward the horses. "Actually, I brought it here so you could take a look and give me some feedback."

"Ha!" Ebeneezer laughed. "Of course you did." He smiled and patted Chandler's shoulder. "So what gives me the pleasure of seeing you here?"

Chandler pushed his glasses up and grinned. "Adventure." He had a look like he was impressed with himself, and Basil snorted, holding down a laugh. Amber felt a twinge of exasperation. For a guy who had barely left his house, he certainly didn't seem very adventuresome.

Ebeneezer raised his eyebrows. "Do tell?" He gestured for Chandler to sit, and the two sat together, leaving the three kids standing behind them watching awkwardly.

Amber shook her head. We're invisible to them. As if we're not worth paying attention to. Part of her felt like just walking out, if they didn't think she was important enough to be involved in their discussions. It was like being with her older siblings all over again.

But then she had a sense of responsibility to her village, her dad, and Old Mr. Thompson and rethought things. Ignore them. They're helping me on a real adventure, whether they know it or not.

Chandler cleared his throat and raised his nose into the air, as if searching for the right words. "We've come across some interesting findings of late, involving goblins and other creatures of note." He raised his eyebrows, looking for a response. "We've come to Wakefield searching for a wizard named Sage. We think he may hold the key to understanding the different types of goblins we've been sighting recently."

"Ah, the goblins." Ebeneezer nodded. "Many have seen them around these parts, none so bold as to come into town, but certainly in the countryside, not too far from here. What sorts of other things have you been seeing? We should compare notes."

Chandler bobbed his head. "Yes, indeed. One of these young ones says a phoenix burned their fields on the coast."

"A phoenix, you say?" Ebeneezer leaned forward.

"Yes." Chandler went on, "They don't actually know if it was a phoenix, a dragon, or something else, but regardless, it's odd—why burn a crop and leave without purpose? From what I understand, it was purely a destructive act."

"Interesting," Ebeneezer said. "I wonder if—"

"And also," Chandler said, "they say their local pixies have all moved on . . . like they had somewhere important to go."

"Ah! I wondered if other magical creatures might be impacted." Ebeneezer pursed his lips. "What else have you learned? Anything else?"

"Yes." Chandler went to a rack on the wall with rolled-up maps and pulled one off, brought it back to the table, and unrolled it. "You see here, we are pretty sure the goblins have generally been coming from the Ancares Mountains." Chandler pointed at the mountains toward the south. "But two of these kids here encountered some goblins north of here with a different pendant, and we're wondering if they might have come from these caves just up here."

"Which means"—Ebeneezer pointed up—"there's more than one source for goblins. Which then blows away my theory that something must have happened at the mountain. Actually—" He rubbed his chin. "This does make sense. We've been hearing of more than goblin sightings over here. There was mention of troll sightings just last week—and I hear that all the way down in Lugo, there's been a dragon who's woken up or something because it's coming every day and eating cows or sheep. It doesn't seem to be focused on people yet, which is good. Although it did kill some men who attacked it."

He paused. "And what do you think Sage will do for you? He's not a warrior, just an old brain-head like us." He knocked his head with his knuckles.

"Yes. We want answers," Chandler replied. "Answers that we believe only a wizard can give."

"Well, I wish I had better news." Ebeneezer shrugged. "But Sage left about a month ago, when the goblins started showing up. He could be anywhere by now."

Chandler frowned. "Any ideas where he might have gone?"

"Well . . ." Ebeneezer thought for a moment. "He's friends with Rochester. Do you know him?"

Chandler shook his head no.

"Well, anyway, Rochester runs the apothecary across town—you know, selling the standard stuff like medicines and herbs and special concoctions. I'm guessing he'll have more information. I don't really know him well myself."

"I imagine his store is closed for the night. Any idea where he'd be right now?" Chandler asked.

"Let's see . . ."

It took them a full two hours before they finally tracked down Rochester. Chandler had spent half an hour showing Ebeneezer his special map. Then they went from building to building in the dark, until finally they found Rochester at a tavern, having a drink with two other men, and asked him about Sage.

Rochester wasn't much help. "I don't know" was his first answer. But after some pressing, he said, "Sage does have a lookout on a mountain far to the east of here that he sometimes goes to. Maybe he's there. But he travels around a lot. He could be anywhere by now."

At the end of it all, the group was exhausted and needed a place to sleep. Chandler took them to an inn where Basil used the money that he'd taken from the goblins, so they could sleep in real beds that night.

Early the next day, the group gathered in the common room of the inn for a light breakfast. They were about to discuss what to do next when in walked Ryder.

Amber blinked a few times. She was so far from Seabrook—having someone from home casually stroll in was jarring. When it clicked in her mind that he was actually there, she stood and called, "Ryder!"

He turned and brightened when he saw her, then gave her a hug. "The one and only." He held her at arm's length. "What have you learned so far?"

"We've learned a lot, but we've also learned that we don't know enough, and we're looking for more help."

"We?" Ryder looked around the table.

Amber introduced Chandler, Theo, and Basil. Ryder politely offered his hand to each of them.

She noticed that Chandler acknowledged Ryder, whereas he hadn't acknowledged her when they'd first met. She wondered what the age cutoff was where that happened—or was it Ryder's mature confidence?

Ryder turned back to Amber. "I have news from the city."

"Do tell?" Chandler happily tapped his fingers together.

Ryder gazed at him curiously, then continued. "They say

that the passages through the mountains further southeast have become more dangerous. And the roads to the south, west, and north are all much safer—for now."

"Interesting." Chandler adjusted his glasses. "That supports our previous theory that the goblins are mostly coming from one location."

"It's not just goblins," Ryder said. "I've talked to couriers who've seen trolls, ogres, and even a dragon. It's like the whole world of dark and magical creatures is waking up."

"Interesting, indeed!" Chandler clapped his hands happily. Amber shook her head at him. How could someone be so happy about evil creatures coming around? Somehow the learning process excited him more than the potential danger.

She cleared her throat. "I came to Wakefield to look for a wizard that Mr. Thompson told me about. But he's not here. We found out he's got another place in the mountains east of here, wherever that is. But we don't even know for sure if he'll be there."

Chandler retrieved one of his maps and laid it on the table. He pointed at a spot far to the southeast of them. "These mountains here are the most likely spot. There are no roads that go straight through them, and it could be anywhere from forty to fifty miles from here. We're talking about a multiple-day journey, just to get there. If you even find it at all—I can't imagine he makes his mountain home easy to find. And as Amber said, he may not even be there."

He sighed and looked at the kids around him. "I'm starting to think this may be too much of a long shot. And I have things to do back in Sanford. My other students are expecting me today, and I have to help my sister move some furniture."

Amber gazed at the map sadly, while the group all looked in silence. Maybe it is a long shot, she thought. Is this what Flurry imagined I'd be doing? Traveling around the countryside looking for a wizard while goblins and trolls lurk around the corners? This is crazy.

Ryder patted her on the back. "Well, at least you tried. Maybe you could figure things out another way?"

Feeling suddenly angry, she pushed his hand away. "No! This is what Mr. Thompson said to do."

Ryder awkwardly stepped back. "Ok. Ok. Don't get excited."

There was an uncomfortable moment where everyone avoided each other's eyes. Ryder broke the silence. "So . . . what's your plan?"

"I don't know." Amber wrung her hands together.

"Hey, all's not lost." Basil grinned. "I'm looking forward

to spending days wandering unknown forests full of goblins and looking for a wizard's hideout. Sounds like fun!"

Ryder laughed. "You have a curious idea of fun."

Amber stood. "You do have a point, Basil. This is the best idea we've had so far, and even if it takes weeks, what else would we do? I can't give up now. My village needs me to figure out what's going on. I'm with you, Basil—I'm doing it, even if some of you can't." She said those last words looking at Chandler.

Basil leaned forward and put his hands on the table. "Fantastic!" He gestured grandly. "It'll be an adventure! And when we run into goblins, we'll have both our weapons to take 'em down."

Amber sighed. She never wanted to see another goblin in her entire life—Basil, on the other hand, seemed eager to run into more. It was as if he wanted to test his fighting abilities. But even though she didn't like the idea of another goblin encounter, the idea of having Basil as a traveling companion lightened her heart.

Theo cleared his throat. "I think I'll go with Chandler. I have lots to do back home."

Basil elbowed him. "Come on, Theo! You can do it. Come have an adventure with us."

Theo shook his head and gave him an evil eye. "Too

dangerous. I'm not cut out for that kind of stuff like you."

Ryder cleared his throat. "I don't know you very well, Theo. I've been our town's courier since I was eleven. You can imagine I've run into all sorts of dangerous things. But what's even more amazing is all the stuff out there in the world—all the things I've seen while out and about. Sometimes you can't learn things from a book."

"I can relate." Amber nodded empathetically. "I don't want to be around danger either, Theo. But my whole village is threatened right now. I can't just do nothing. I'm sure you feel the same."

Theo gazed at her for a moment, then gave a slow nod. "Ok. I'll stick it out." He turned to look at Ryder. "And I *have* left Sanford. But I admit, I'm not normally a traveling sort." His voice wavered slightly, sounding like he was trying to be brave but was actually scared out of his wits.

Basil punched him in the arm playfully. "Alright! This is gonna be way better. I know you're already packed but you'd better get yourself some kind of weapon."

Theo gulped, then nodded. "I'm no good with swords, but I've used a bow and arrows before. I could probably hit a target if I practiced a bit. Let's see if we can find one around town."

Ryder tapped his fingers on the table. "Amber, I'll let

your parents know what you're doing. They'll be happy to know you've found some friends. When I'm passing back through later this week, I'll keep my eyes peeled for you."

"You don't feel like joining us, do you?" She smiled at him.

Ryder squirmed and twisted a piece of rolled up parchment in his hands. "I have all my duties to take care of. Otherwise I would."

"Huh." Amber shrugged, disappointed, and turned away.

Chandler looked around the table. "Well, I'm proud of you kids. You're very brave. But what will you do if you run into goblins? Are you sure you can handle them? I'm not so sure this is a good idea."

He noticed their faces turn down and said, "Ok, how about this? Promise me you'll stay clear of any goblins you find. If you see tracks, go a different way. Any whiff of danger, and you hide. Can you do that for me?"

"Yes!" Amber and Basil said in unison and then grinned at each other. They turned to Theo.

"Yeah. Yes. Ok." Theo said, as if his mind was a hundred miles away.

"Ok then, it's settled." Basil stood and patted Theo on the shoulder. "We'll get Theo a bow and get going today." He turned to Chandler. "Can you tell Theo's parents and mine?"

Chandler nodded, then immediately turned away and began putting his things together. Not one for the emotional stuff like goodbyes, Amber thought. She looked at Ryder, who seemed preoccupied.

Looks like I can't count on him. I wonder why he's so stuck on doing his courier duties when this is clearly more important?

She brushed the thought aside and began focusing on preparing for their trip. Now that they were planning for possible weeks, there would be more details to work out.

They left Wakefield within an hour, taking a less-traveled road due east. There were still people on it from time to time, but not busy like the other roads going into Wakefield. It was a pleasant day, and Amber was happy to have her traveling companions.

At first, she felt awkward around Basil and Theo—like an outsider. They obviously knew each other extremely well. But then Theo rode next to her and started asking questions.

"What's it like living by the sea?"

"Oh, I'm not sure how to compare it with your town, but our whole lives revolve around it. We fish there, and swim there, and spend a lot of time out on it. We do have some farming, though, and hunting. I've done all of them—that's our way there. We make sure all the kids know all the trades, so when they're old enough, they can pick."

"What are you going to pick?" Theo asked.

"Not sure. I have a way with plants. I can get plants to grow that no one else seems to be able to, and I seem to have a way of making crops thrive. So most of the town thinks that's what I should do."

"But what do *you* think?" Theo asked.

"Well, I do love gardening, but . . ." Amber trailed off.

"I knew there'd be more," he said after a moment. "Otherwise, you wouldn't be out here looking for a wizard."

"Yeah, that's right. I love reading and figuring out riddles and things. And I also love tending plants. And then there's this side of me that wants to get out in the world and make a difference—do something grand. Do you think I can somehow do all that?"

"Maybe so," Theo replied. "Although last time I checked, plants don't grow on horses!" He laughed, and Amber laughed with him.

Basil chimed in, "You could wander around and plant things wherever you go. We have an old story about a guy who did that hundreds of years ago, and that's why we have the fruit trees we have in our town."

"Interesting," she said, then turned to Theo. "How about you? Do the people of your town want you to figure out your profession at your age?"

"Oh sure. But they always figured I'd do some sort of clerical work—like things that involve reading and writing, since I've always got my nose in a book and I don't ever leave town."

"Except for now," she said.

"Well, yeah, except for now." He patted his horse's neck. "Butterfly is finally putting some miles in! I suppose it's all Basil's fault. He's always out and about on some adventure, and since we're best friends—"

"My fault?" Basil frowned. "Come on, Theo! Don't sound so whiny. Every time I drag you out, you're glad afterward."

"I don't know if I'd say that . . ." Theo shook his head.

"Not true! Why do you always have to judge me?" Basil's voice took on an edge. "Look, Theo. You've been needing to get out of town for nearly half a year now! You were holed up all winter long and never once left. Now it's finally spring—it's time to get out and smell some flowers, see some sights. Meet some goblins!"

He said that last part in a sort of spooky voice, and

Theo's face fell.

"Just kidding!" Basil said quickly. "It'll be fun." But Theo looked upset, and they all grew quiet.

Amber looked at Basil, annoyed. "Basil, too much."

After a moment he said, "Well, anyway, if we do run into goblins, Theo, stay back and use that bow we bought for you. Amber's a fantastic shot, and I can handle at least one or two with my sword. No need for you to put yourself in danger."

Theo nodded and looked a bit pale. Amber hoped that if they did run into goblins, Theo would know what to do.

They camped that night near the road. Amber set up a target and helped Theo with his archery techniques. He wasn't very good to start, but could at least hit the target by the time it grew dark.

"You'll get there," Basil said encouragingly.

Theo gave him a dirty look. "I told you I'm not good."

"No, you're fine. You just need more practice."

Theo sighed and put the bow and arrows next to his mat.

Although they didn't sleep as well as the previous night when they were snug in beds, the crisp spring air revitalized them, and they felt energized when they awoke.

Around noon, they came to a small village named Mira.

They asked about the best route to the potential mountain Sage's lookout could be on.

"I once heard that it's that way," a woman told them, pointing to the mountains in the distance to their east. They tried asking as many people as they could, but that was the closest they got to real directions.

They realized with all the maps they'd been looking at the last day, they hadn't had the wherewithal to bring one with them. Theo had brought some parchment and started drawing his own map. He looked at another map from a local person, then copied it and filled in a bit more detail.

The best route, from what they could gather, was a road that would eventually turn into a path not fit for a wagon but would probably be fine for their horses. They were warned that there were no other towns or villages that way—just forest and mountains for hundreds of miles.

As soon as they left Mira heading east, there were no people to be seen anywhere. Not only that, the road was in ill repair, with deep holes from horses' hooves made during muddy days, causing them to travel much slower than before to keep their horses from hurting themselves on the uneven ground.

The road quickly became a trail with branches growing into the path and blocking their way, as well as the occasional fallen tree they would have to go around. It was still faster than going off into the dense forest, though, so they kept on.

And although they'd promised earlier that day to hide if they saw goblins, they didn't have a moment to think when a group of goblins suddenly came running at them with swords drawn, ready to kill.

Chapter 12

The Courier's Search

RYDER TRAVELED ON THE WELL-WORN ROAD to Seabrook atop Rocky's brown-and-white back, deep in thought. He barely noticed his surroundings, having done this ride so many times before. He didn't read the signs to pick his path or pay attention to the peaceful sounds of the countryside around him.

He wondered why Amber was going out of her way to find a wizard—but also felt like he should be doing the same. Was something big really going on . . . and were there more than a few goblins coming out of their caves?

The road turned to the last little stretch toward

Seabrook, and Ryder kicked his horse to go a little faster. When he arrived, he delivered the four letters he'd been carrying from Lugo. The same four people every time: three with family members in the large city, and the mayor of the town sending correspondence again. Maybe he was telling them about the phoenix, Ryder thought.

He stopped at Amber's house to give her parents the update about her, then went back to his home for a quiet night with his dad.

The next day in Seabrook, he was too busy with his normal duties to think any more about the phoenix, the wizard, Amber, and what he could or should do—if anything. It wasn't until he'd gathered the last of his mail and set off west toward the coastal town of Strathmere that it all started to stir within him again.

Of course they could use his powers, he reasoned. But was he ready to reveal them to the rest of the world? He remembered Amber saying the pixies were a big factor in her decision to head out and wondered if there were still any around.

He entered Strathmere and delivered the mail. When the last letter was delivered, he went to Mrs. Rugsby's old rugged house and knocked on the door. If there was anyone in that little village who'd know how to find pixies, it would be her. She always had her nose in everyone's business, whether they liked it or not.

A middle-aged woman opened the door. She was plain, with a large awkward nose and slitted eyes that darted around. "Yes? How can I help you, Ryder?" She stood in her doorway, one hand on her rotund hip and an apron around her waist.

"Hi, Mrs. Rugsby." Ryder smiled. "I'm wondering if you know of any pixies living in these parts, and if so, if you would direct me where I can find them?"

Mrs. Rugsby frowned. "Pixies? What on earth would you want to find *them* for?"

Ryder didn't answer but just continued to smile. The less she knew, the less rumors she'd spread about it.

After a pause, when she could tell she wouldn't get Ryder to say anything, she said, "There's a small group of kids who sometimes go out and talk with some west of here. I've never seen them myself. They never come into town."

"Which kids?" Ryder asked.

"Oh, your best bet is Sammy. He'll know."

"Thank you so much." Ryder nodded his head in respect.

"What are you looking for pixies for, anyway?" she asked politely.

"Oh, it's nothing." He knew instantly that Mrs. Rugsby would take that to mean the exact opposite. Which, he supposed, was true. "Thanks again!" He waved and headed back down the street.

He found Sammy and the kids playing a game with a ball made of straw. They kicked it over a waist-high net back and forth to each other without using their hands. Ryder watched them for a bit, smiling. It looked like the purpose of the game was just to have fun and keep the ball going, not score on the other side. He made a mental note to remember to try it later, then said, "Sammy, got a minute?"

Sammy and the other children were quick to show Ryder the pixies, so all six kids wrapped up their game and walked with him to the west edge of town and into the dense forest. The whole way they laughed and joked with each other, making a great racket.

I guess there's no sneaking up on pixies anyway, Ryder thought. "How much longer is it?"

"Oh, about fifteen minutes." Sammy skipped and whacked at a bush with a stick he'd picked up. "They always meet us at the clearing by the pond."

Fifteen minutes was like no time at all to kids playing tag along the way. The pond was teeming with little flying bugs, and frogs and turtles were sunbathing all along its banks. All the kids but Sammy ran to the pond and started catching frogs. Sammy smiled at Ryder and whistled loudly, then called, "Ruffles! Where are you?"

He walked around the clearing and whistled again. The sound of the other children laughing when one of them accidentally stepped into the pond echoed through the trees. Then a small pixie in a bright-green jacket and tightfitting brown pants flew toward them.

"Ruffles!" Sammy's eyes brightened. Then he frowned. "What's wrong?"

The small pixie looked worried. "Sammy, we may be leaving soon."

"Why?" Sammy's shoulders deflated.

The pixie looked behind Sammy to Ryder and pointed. "Who's that?"

"I'm Ryder. I have a question for you. A friend of mine was talking to the pixies from Seabrook and—"

Ruffles cut him off. "Seabrook?"

Ryder paused. "Yes . . . that's what I said—"

"Those pixies are here right now. But they're not staying."

"Really?" Ryder raised his eyebrows. "I wonder if the ones who talked with Amber might be able to give me some advice."

Ruffles shrugged. "I can ask them." He looked back at Sammy, then at Ryder again, and darted off into the trees.

Sammy shrugged at Ryder. "They're sometimes like that. Who knows what they're up to?"

Ryder nodded and waited. Sammy stood for a moment, then said, "If it's all the same to you, I'm going to see what my friends have caught."

"Sure, go ahead." Ryder smiled and gestured for the boy to go.

The wait for Ruffles felt long and painful. The sound of the children laughing and screaming lifted Ryder's spirits a bit, but he still felt off, like he was missing something important.

When Ruffles finally returned, it was with one other pixie, a young girl wearing a spiffy white-and-blue outfit and looking reluctant to be there. Ryder talked quickly. "My name's Ryder, a friend of Amber. Are you from Seabrook? Do you know Amber?"

Instantly the pixie perked up. "Amber?"

Ryder hadn't spoken to pixies for what felt like half his life, but he did remember that you had to keep them engaged and interested. "Do you know who talked to her before she left Seabrook? I want to talk to them."

"Why is that?" The pixie looked a bit mischievous, and

Ryder started remembering again why he'd stopped bothering to talk with them. Even though they seemed to know a lot of stuff, wrenching it out was always painful and difficult.

"I was just with her, and she has a question. But first, I need to know who she talked to. Do you know the pixie who spoke with her last?"

The pixie nodded. "I do. The name's Flurry. What's Amber's question?"

Ryder thought quickly. He'd have to make something up. At least he found what seemed like a pixie who knew a thing or two. "She's off looking for a wizard, and it seems like an impossible task. She's wondering if that's what you wanted her to do?"

The pixie looked at Ryder for a moment, then said, "You're wondering why I sent her. You wonder if you should go too."

He looked at her in shock. How did she figure all that out from his awkward question? He stammered. "Umm . . ."

"Everyone needs help. Even you, Ryder. You can't travel alone forever." There was an awkward pause, and the pixie sighed. "Tell Amber when you see her that it's worse than we thought. It's all connected. She's needed more than any of us knew."

"But why her?" He peered into the small pixie's eyes, tiny little dots as blue and clear as the sky.

Flurry grinned and looked mischievous again. "Wouldn't *you* want to know, Mr. Ryder, with all sorts of hidden powers. You could be a big help to her, you know."

She began to jitter up and around excitedly. "Do tell her when you see her that we're fine—but still on the move. And I bet she still hasn't worn that hat!"

Ryder furrowed his brow, then smiled. "I will tell her. When I see her. Thank you, Flurry."

The two pixies flew up and away, leaving Ryder to his thoughts. The pixie knew of his hidden power. And he so badly wanted to use it. Maybe he really should have joined Amber when he had the chance. But how could he find her? She was headed deep into mountains without any proper roads. His best bet would probably be to seek her out at one of the cities.

He stretched and walked back to the village without saying goodbye to the kids. He was good at finding people. That was his job, after all. And he'd found her before.

He could keep doing his courier duties and travel around the countryside. In the process, he could keep an ear out for more information. And he could start with Chandler, in Sanford. Chandler seemed to have lots of ideas.

✳ ✳ ✳

The late afternoon light was creating a beautiful red glow on the ancient trees and large rocks, and Ryder sighed contentedly. As usual, much of his pleasure as a delivery person was the journey in between stops.

He sighted Sanford in the distance. Perfect timing. As usual. He spurred Rocky forward, and they trotted past the large wooden gates. He noticed four guards were there now, rather than the usual one guard. Or even none, just a year ago. He nodded to them and headed toward the courier hostel where all the delivery people would stay.

Every town had one, even the smaller villages, although those would have more like a spare room next to a common hall of some sort. He fed and watered Rocky, then asked the other couriers the whereabouts of Chandler's shop.

He grabbed a quick bite to eat, walked down the streets, and within a few minutes was standing in front of Chandler's two-story yellow building. He walked right in. A bell attached to the door handle rang as Ryder opened it.

Chandler sat at a back table with an oil lamp and looked up. At first, he looked puzzled, then he smiled, "Ryder! What brings you through these parts? Any news from our friends?"

Ryder strode over to the table and sat down. "No news.

But I did a little exploring of my own and talked to some pixies. Turns out, they think it's worse than we thought. They're very cryptic, so I don't actually know what that means, but it sounded like they're worried and on the move."

"Interesting." Chandler took off his glasses and fiddled with them. "Anything else? What are you thinking?"

"I want to find Amber and the others."

"Well, that will be next to impossible." Chandler shook his head. "They're off in the mountains somewhere, maybe even found the wizard by now. How on earth do you think you can track them down?"

"I'm pretty good at finding people. But I don't know. Maybe I should wait somewhere for them to return. I also think we need to learn more. The pixies said it was more serious than they'd thought. I wanted to talk with you, see what you think."

Chandler smiled and looked proud of himself. "Of course you do, my boy. Well." He looked around the room for a moment. "I don't think the answers are here." His voice trailed off. "If we want to find more answers, they'll be in Lugo. We can do proper research in a real library." The scholarly man looked surprised at himself for suggesting it, then straightened his composure.

Ryder stared into space. He wasn't much of a reader, and

going to a library seemed like the last thing to do when in a rush. But the thought of learning more did sound appealing. "Do you really think we can learn what we need to know in a library?"

"Of course, my boy. Of course! This book collection I have here is a tiny scratch compared to what we can find there."

Ryder looked skeptical, and Chandler's eyes gained some urgency. "If you want me to come with you, it will have to wait a week or so. But listen . . . It's not just the books. It's the people. People who are educated properly. People who live in a bigger city and have exposure to more of the happenings around the country. If we want answers, they're not here, they're there."

There was a moment of silence and both of them looked at each other with understanding. Ryder cleared his throat. "When's the soonest you can leave?"

Chapter 13

The Lookout

AT LEAST THREE GOBLINS CHARGED down the narrow path toward Amber, Theo, and Basil, swords raised and yelling in their raspy guttural voices. Theo screamed and fumbled for his bow. Basil drew his sword and spurred his horse toward the goblins yelling, "Attack!"

Amber quickly pulled her bow off her shoulder and drew an arrow in one fluid movement, releasing an arrow into a goblin before Basil reached them. Without thinking, she aimed for the necks, since that was the weak spot on the goblin she'd fought the last time. Sure enough, the goblin dropped instantly while the others scrambled around.

The path was too narrow for her to fire a second shot with Basil charging down on his horse, so she tried walking Buttercup a few steps to the left into the bushes for a better angle.

From the side, she could make out three goblins running toward them. Basil was charging at the closest one, so she aimed at the next closest one and released. Again, a perfect shot. The goblin toppled to the ground instantly and didn't move.

Basil leaned over and used his sword to stab the first goblin, slashing at its arm while it also managed to hit his right leg. Basil continued toward the fourth goblin and plunged his sword into its chest. Unfortunately, the impact threw him from his horse and into the bushes. Storm stopped and looked around awkwardly.

The last goblin continued to charge toward Amber. She drew another arrow and let it fly right as the goblin was about to reach her. It hit the goblin in the chest, slowing it down but not dropping it like the first two. The goblin jumped at her with his sword.

Buttercup reared up in fear, kicking the goblin in the face. The goblin was knocked terribly but still managed to grab the reins and hold on while it swung with its rusty old blade. Buttercup jumped and reared again, trying to shake it off, but instead of shaking off the goblin, Amber was tossed to the ground.

She rolled and grabbed for an arrow, but they'd fallen out of her quiver and were strewn all over. She tried grasping for an arrow as Buttercup continued to jump and kick with the goblin holding on tightly. Panic welled up inside her heart. She was completely defenseless without her arrows.

Then she heard a *thwack!* and turned. It was Theo, who had finally managed to pull his bow off his shoulder. He'd sent an arrow straight into the goblin, amid all the bucking and movement, and the goblin released its grasp and fell. Amber got to her hands and knees and scrambled across the ground toward some arrows. She quickly notched one and looked around.

The fourth goblin struggled weakly, and she released the arrow into it. The creature stopped moving and lay still. All four goblins lay on the ground motionless. She watched the surrounding forest, waiting for another goblin to pounce. Her breathing was rugged and wild, and she turned around, watching carefully, an arrow notched at the ready.

All remained quiet and calm for a full minute. As a gentle breeze blew into her face she suddenly realized Basil was nowhere to be seen. "Basil! Where are you?"

"Uuuuugh!" A groan came from the bushes beyond the

last goblin, and Amber went running. Basil was tangled up in a bush with scrapes down his face and a big cut in his leg from the goblin's sword. His curly hair was full of twigs and leaves, and his pant leg had a big opening in it.

She helped him stand with one hand, keeping her bow with a notched arrow in the other, and they looked around together. The four goblins remained motionless. Theo sat on his horse, holding an arrow notched, watching the dense forest and shaking. They all stood at the ready, watching for movements from the four goblins on the ground and listening for sounds from the surrounding woods.

Finally, Amber relaxed her bow somewhat. "I think we got them all." She turned to Basil. "Are you ok?"

He suddenly felt the pain of his injuries, now that the adrenaline was wearing off. He grabbed his right shoulder and winced. "Ow. My arm. I must have pulled it when I got yanked off my horse." He moved it around in circles carefully.

"You're bleeding," she said, pointing to his leg.

He looked down, surprised. It didn't appear deep, but blood was staining his pants from a long slice down the thigh. "Oh. I didn't even know I got that!"

She felt his shoulder tenderly, and then they walked over to Buttercup so Amber could get her medical kit. She put a salve on his shoulder to help it heal quickly and rubbed some herbs on the leg wound, then bandaged it up.

"Not too deep at all," Amber said. "You're lucky."

Basil smiled as he winced.

The three went about pulling the goblins off the trail and seeing what items they had. All in all, there was more money, two more pendants with the mountain design, and weapons—mostly junky scimitars, except one short sword in decent condition that Theo decided to keep.

"I feel naked with only a bow," Theo said. "I know it's not a nice sword, and I may never use this, but it's something." He strapped it onto his waist. "Basil, you'll have to show me a thing or two. It's been a long time since anyone taught me how to use these things."

Basil held his hand out, and Theo gave him the short sword. He felt the balance of it, then handed it back. "Can do. It's not a good blade, but it'll work. I could use some new training myself. If I'm going to be doing attacks from a horse, I think I should be using a longer sword. I think that's why I got thrown—in order to do any damage I had to lean in really far, and it got stuck."

"Where will you get one out here?" Theo asked.

Basil shrugged. "No idea. But let's keep our eyes peeled." He patted his short sword strapped to his left side. "This is a beautiful blade, though. I don't think I would ever want to part with it."

"I just hope we don't run into any more goblins," Amber said. "I'm already sick of killing. I've helped kill six goblins in the last three days. Not what I expected when I started out on this journey."

The boys nodded. Nobody could disagree with that.

Throughout the rest of the day, they were tense and alert. Even Theo talked only when necessary as they traveled single file down the narrow trail through the dense forest.

At one point, Amber was in the rear and noticed a flitting motion ahead of her. It gave her a start, but then she realized that in the quiet, Theo seemed to be somehow attractive to the birds. They fluttered around him, even landing on his shoulders and head from time to time.

I wonder what that's about, she thought. Animals seem to love him. He must have a gift.

It started feeling dark far before it actually was, with all the tall trees blocking much of the sun. The forest didn't feel friendly enough for them to stay the night, but they knew they needed to sleep soon.

"Let's see if there's any clear ground up that way. It looks promising." Basil pointed to their left, up the mountain.

The group cautiously left the trail and went directly up

the hill toward a rock outcropping. It turned out to be a small clearing, but the rocks were out in the open and had a vantage point of the forest below. So they set up their camp for the night, with their backs to the rocks and a view of the sunset.

Basil pulled out a needle and thread to patch the gaping hole in his pants as Theo and Amber pulled out some of the fresh food to cook over a fire. With a warm fire, food in their bellies, and a view of the sunset, the weary travelers' mood picked up, and they enjoyed one another's company.

"Hey, Amber," Theo said, "which cup has the rock?" He'd set three drinking cups upside down on a flat rock.

"That one." She pointed to the middle one.

"Good." Theo lifted the middle cup. "Now watch the cups. Don't lose focus on the one with the rock." He proceeded to move the cups around quickly. It was all she could do to follow the cup with the rock. Finally, he stopped moving the cups. "Ok, which cup is it in?"

"That one!" She pointed to the cup on the right. Theo lifted the cup, but no rock was in it. "Hmm." She scratched her head. "Ok, that one!" She pointed at the next one. Again, the cup had no rock. "That one?"

Theo lifted the third cup, and no rock was in it. He and Basil started to laugh.

"Where is it?"

Theo smiled at her. "You really don't see it?" His voice sounded a little odd.

"No," Amber said, then looked at Theo's face. The rock was in his lips! "Good trick!" She smiled with admiration, then changed the subject. "Hey, nice shot back there. I was really worried about that goblin. It was right on top of me."

"Yeah, thanks." Theo said. "I definitely don't use a bow like you, but it all came back to me when I saw you in trouble."

"Let's hope you don't have to use it again," said Amber.

"There are worse things . . . like studying about leeches with Chandler!" He gave Basil a wink.

Basil gestured as if pulling a leech off his arm and smiled. "Who knew there were fifty different medical benefits of leeches?"

Theo chuckled. "There's at least one they didn't mention in the textbook—helping you fall asleep when you study about them!" They all laughed.

Theo filled in more of his map, and Amber stared at it with interest, thinking of how far she'd traveled. My village must be way over there, past those far mountains. I hope they're ok and have no more issues with the phoenix.

The stars came out, and Theo told some stories about

the constellations. The great dragon who came and devoured the sea creature. The brave hero who was riding a bear. She was fascinated. She knew some stories from constellations but very few, and she was eager to hear more.

That night they went to bed happy and glad for each other's company. The next morning, Basil nudged Amber as she slept. "Look at that!" he whispered.

She rubbed her eyes. He was pointing into the sky. There in the distance, a large red dragon flew over the forest below.

"Wow!" she whispered. "A dragon!" Its red-and-yellow body glistened in the early sun as it flew over the land. They watched in fascination when it dove down.

"Ooh!" they all said in unison. They waited with breaths held, then the dragon rose above the trees holding a bighorn sheep in its talons. It flew off toward their left and disappeared from their view around the mountain.

"Whoa!" Theo said. "Unbelievable."

"I never thought I'd see a dragon in my whole life!" Amber thought of the description of the creature that had burned the field back in Seabrook. Definitely smaller than that large creature! That dragon was more like the size of twenty or even forty cows, not three or four. It had to be a phoenix that burned the field. But why? I hope Sage has some answers.

They packed up and continued on their way. "Let's go already!" Basil called and trotted off ahead. The others rode after him but soon realized they had absolutely no idea where to go. They rode around a mountain and saw another three to choose from. They took a break and examined the mountains for clues.

"Do we have more information to go on?" Theo sounded discouraged. "If we don't know where we're going exactly, we could wander these goblin-infested forests for months! Are you sure Sage is on one of these mountains?"

"I don't know," Amber admitted. "This is starting to feel like a long shot."

"Yeah. It is." Theo pulled out his map. "I feel like we're wasting our time here. There are more mountains than map space! And even if we do find the right mountain with Sage's lookout, *and* happen to find his secret hiding spot on that mountain, what if he isn't there?"

Amber felt a lump in her throat. Maybe Theo was right. Were they wasting their time?

Theo wrung his hands. "Basil, why did you drag me out here? There are goblins and even dragons! I can barely use a bow well enough to be any real help. I'm useless anyway."

"Not true!" Basil stood with his fists on his hips. "I know you're not a fighter, but that's not all we need! Your map is helping us track where we're going."

Theo rolled his map up and tapped it into his other hand assertively. "But look at us. We're wandering around searching for a hard-to-find lookout in the middle of who-knows-where and constantly in danger. Is this really worth it?" He turned to Amber. "Are you sure Sage is going to be worth all this trouble?"

Amber lowered her eyes. "No. I'm not sure. I don't know anything about him."

"See? Once again, Basil, you've pushed me past the point of reason. This time it's gone too far. There's no way we're finding this wizard, and even if we do, what if he doesn't help?"

Basil pointed his finger at Theo. "Here we go again. Whine, whine, whine. Why can't you just look on the bright side of things for once? Maybe we *won't* find the wizard, but isn't it nice to be outside in the fresh air?"

Theo stared him in the eyes. "Basil, I had to kill a goblin. This isn't for me. Don't you get it? Finding the wizard is futile anyway, and there's more danger than ever out here in the wilderness. This isn't for me. You know that."

Theo sighed as he saw Basil's face soften. "Listen. We gave it a chance. I'm not done helping. But let's be smart about things, not just go rushing off on some fool's errand."

Basil kicked a rock uncomfortably and avoided looking at Theo in the eyes. "I don't know. I guess you're right."

Amber's heart dropped. It was one thing to have Theo losing hope but Basil as well? She felt tears welling up. She turned away and put her hands in her pockets.

Basil sighed and put his hand on Theo's shoulder. "Ok, Theo. I'm willing to admit this adventure seems foolish. We could just wait for Sage back in Wakefield. I don't want to put you in any more danger."

"Thanks, Basil." Theo smiled.

Basil turned. "What about you, Amber?"

Amber felt tears welling up. Would she keep going alone? Was it even worth it? "I . . . I don't know. I guess . . . if you're planning on going back to Wakefield . . . we can always hope Sage will show up there."

But even as she said the words her heart sank. "Can you give me a few minutes to think about it?"

Basil and Theo nodded, and Amber walked to a small clearing, with the mountains in the distance. Could Sage be on one of those mountains? So close, but we've no way of knowing. It felt futile. If only there was some magic way they could find Sage's lookout . . .

"Wait!" Amber ran back to Theo and Basil. "I was told to only use this when I'm desperate. But this is starting to feel that way." She pulled the small, white pixie-enchanted stone from her pocket.

"What's that?" Theo and Basil asked in unison.

She lifted the rock by its attached string and watched it spin. "This . . . is an enchanted rock. I can ask it where to go, and it will point us in the right direction. I can only ask it one thing. It was a gift from the pixies. We can ask it where to find Sage."

"And if Sage is clear across the continent?" Theo asked.

"Well, at least we'll know we're wasting our time here." Amber shrugged. "What do you think? Is this a good time to use the rock?"

"Definitely!" Theo replied. "I can't believe you have something that amazing in your pocket! I don't think we'll be able to find Sage without it. Let's do it."

"Ok," she said. "Here goes."

"Wait!" Theo frowned in thought. "Make sure you frame what you're going to say well. If you just tell it to point us toward him and he's halfway around the world, we'll have no idea. If it only works on one thing, we want to be sure what we ask it."

"Sounds good."

They discussed a few variations on what to say, then she finally turned to the rock. "Enchanted rock, lead us to the place where we can encounter the wizard Sage the soonest."

Theo gave her a grin and a big thumbs-up. The rock spun slowly on its string, then settled with the black notch pointed toward the mountain on their far right.

"Looks like this way!" Amber's eyes sparkled. "Let's hope it's this mountain here, not ten mountains behind it!" She felt a lightness return to her heart, and somehow the day seemed brighter.

Basil and Theo laughed, and they mounted their horses. With no trail and lots of thick underbrush, the going was slow. They tried finding the best trail while also keeping in the general direction given by the stone. At one point, as afternoon was growing hot and weary, they discussed options.

"I think we need to decide whether it's this mountain or the next." Basil paused to wipe leaves and twigs out of his hair. "Because if it's the next, it'll be a lot quicker if we go around the mountain rather than over it."

"That's true." Theo unrolled the map and drew another mountain. "And there's really no risk, because the rock will let us know. As we go around, if we're supposed to go up to the top of that mountain, it'll continue to point to the top."

"Yes, that makes sense," Amber said. "You seem to be good at figuring out stuff like this."

"Oh yeah," Theo beamed. "We do riddles all the time back home. This is just like a riddle."

"Riddles? I like the sound of that." She thought about how different her life would have been if she'd grown up with Basil and Theo in their larger town.

As they traveled around the mountain, sure enough the rock pointed to the next mountain, so Theo's idea saved them the trouble of crossing directly over it. But the going was slow, and they decided to camp again that night, before it got too dark.

The next morning they set out again. It was cold and windy, and the horses seemed to be moving at a snail's pace. As they moved around the next mountain, the stone pointed up to the top, and the trio's mood picked up, knowing they were finally on the last mountain of their journey.

They stopped for lunch, then continued ascending the mountain. The path grew quite steep at some points, still passable for their horses, although a few times they had to walk and scramble up the slope.

After an hour, Theo pointed up the mountain excitedly. "Look! A building!"

They stared in awe. All the way up this rough climb, in the middle of vast stretches of wilderness, someone had built a structure on the top of the mountain.

"How did they build that up here?" Basil shook his head in amazement.

"Donkeys?" Theo wondered aloud.

"Huh. I don't know. It's not only steep, it's all the way out here in the middle of nowhere. I can't think of any normal way someone would build this. Maybe it was magic?"

Close to an hour later, they rounded the last bend in the trail and saw the house before them. It stood at the summit of the mountain, with a full view in every direction.

The house was a perfect hexagon—with tall windows on all six sides and supported by many legs, raised about eight feet above ground. There was a wooden ladder hanging down from the middle of it to the ground below.

"Look at those windows!" Amber said. "They're so big! I've never seen a window like that, ever."

They weren't fully floor-to-ceiling but may as well have been. They started a few feet up and reached high with an arch at the top, around eight feet tall and four feet wide, with two on each wall all the way around.

"This definitely has the look of a wizard's place." Basil stood with his fists on his hips, admiring the handiwork. "I can't imagine anyone else living out here having such a magnificent building."

He turned to Amber. "I think we've found Sage. What does the stone say?"

"This is it." She nodded and felt a little thrill of exhilaration, her thoughts spinning. "Let's hope he's friendly—and can give us some helpful information."

The three travelers tied their horses to some trees in the shade and took off the saddles, then walked over to the building. The only way they could see to get up to the house was directly underneath, using a sturdy wooden ladder attached to a trap door in the floor.

They looked at one another, and Basil started climbing up. "Wait here. In case I have to come down quickly."

Amber and Theo nodded and watched him climb. He got to the top and turned the lever to release the door. It opened upward, so he slowly raised it and peered in. He took another step and stuck more of his head in.

"Hello!" he called. When there was silence, he looked down the ladder at the others. "Come on up!"

Amber and Theo climbed the ladder to the main floor. Before even noticing what was inside, the vista from the building was unbelievable—stretching in every direction as far as the eye could see. Amber wondered if the haze she saw to the north was the sea, near where she lived. It had to be fifty miles away but seemed nearly visible from the lookout.

"It's so green!" Theo said quietly.

The mountains rolled in every direction, and a variety of lush greens filled the land. To the west, mountains and forest turned into plains, far in the distance.

After a moment, Basil said, "Look at this!"

Amber was torn from the view and looked at the table where Basil was pointing. It was a map of the entire land, even bigger than what they'd seen at Chandler's place. They peered at it and found where they were, then noticed a number of red putty globs placed in locations all around, mostly to the southeast.

"That's my village!" Amber pointed at a spot to the northwest by the sea that had a small red putty marker on it. There were markers on all the villages of the coast within twenty miles east of hers. It's like they're targeting the sea towns, Amber thought.

After examining the map for a while, the group looked around. There were a few bookcases and dressers, some large chests, and another table with four chairs. A basic cot was in one corner, and in the center was a small fireplace with a metal tube that ran up through the ceiling. In front of the fireplace was a comfy chair and some furs on the ground.

"Hey, look at that!" Amber pointed toward the ceiling at

another trap door with a ring.

"Here!" Basil picked up a stick with a hook at the end and lifted it up to the ring. He pulled and a folding staircase came down halfway. He grabbed the bottom stair, and it reached the ground perfectly. The stairs led into a dark chamber above, but it was still light enough to see a whole other space.

Basil stepped up the stairs carefully and peered in. "Magic!"

Amber and Theo climbed up after him. Although the slanted roof made the ceiling angle down to six feet on the edges, it still felt spacious. It was much clearer now that the building was in the shape of a hexagon—six angled skylight windows were built into each section of the ceiling. They were a foot wide and four feet tall, enough to let in plenty of light to see the room and its contents.

A large, black cauldron sat in one corner, and one of the walls was lined with hundreds of vials of all sorts of shapes and colors. They had labels but most weren't in a language that any of them recognized. They looked like ancient runes from another age.

Theo peered at a vial of purple liquid with the label *Protection*. He tapped the glass gingerly and the liquid sloshed about like thick sauce. "This sure seems like a wizard's hideaway. I wonder who owns all this?

As if on cue, they heard a voice behind them. "Ahem!"

They jumped and turned to see a short, old man with a sparse black beard, bright-yellow billowy shirt, and black pants standing behind them, watching them sternly.

"U-u-um." Theo stammered. "Nice place?"

Chapter 14

Forming a Plan

THEY ALL STOOD WATCHING EACH OTHER in silence for a moment. The trio was too shocked to say anything . . . the old man appeared to be assessing them sharply.

Finally, Theo spoke. "Are you Sage? We've been told to find you."

The stern brown eyes softened, and the old man smiled. "Indeed? Now who would do such a thing?" He spoke with an accent none of them recognized, as if from a far-off land.

He was exotic—slightly slanted eyes and darker skinned than those in their communities. His jacket had an unusual design unlike any they'd ever seen, barely perceptible swirling circles, with six large fabric buttons in the front and sleeves that billowed.

Amber felt her tongue finally come unglued. "It was Old Mr. Thompson. He said you might be able to help."

"Ah!" Sage nodded slowly. "Well then, you'll want to get the tour!"

Theo looked at Amber with wide eyes and mouthed, *That was easy!*

She smiled and followed Sage downstairs to the main floor. The first thing he showed them was a large black telescope they hadn't noticed earlier. "This magnifies what you're seeing ninety times," he said proudly. "One of the best of its kind." He glanced at Amber. "The spyglasses used by your folks in Seabrook only magnify fifteen to twenty." He patted it happily.

She watched him in awe, not because of his fantastic telescope, but because he knew where she was from.

That made her wonder: *Was that because I mentioned Old Mr. Thompson? But he lives a long way from Seabrook. Just what sorts of things do wizards know? If he can know things about me before he's even met me, he must know a lot about everyone.*

"Let's see," Sage mumbled, making a few adjustments to some knobs on the telescope. "There! Take a look."

The wizard stood up and gestured with an open hand.

Amber peered into the glass and gasped. "Look at all the goblins!" She turned to Sage. "What are they doing?"

As the other two peered through the scope, Sage said, "As far as I can surmise, they have come out of their mountain home and are preparing for some rather unappealing effort against humanity. You see those large tents?"

Basil squinted through the scope. "The big brown ones?"

"Indeed." Sage gestured purposely with his hands. "Goblins tend to live in caves, and they very much don't like to be in the sun for long. By the size of those tents, I believe they are gearing up for a longer excursion out among civilization."

"War?" Theo asked.

"Indubitably." Sage nodded grandly. "But against whom and to what purpose, I haven't a clue. You see, goblins don't have any real desire to live in human cities, so why bother attacking them unless it's part of a bigger plan, with more moving pieces."

"What are all those red marks you've made on your map?" Amber asked.

"Ah, yes." Sage walked over to the table. "I've been tracking significant occurrences of an unusual nature."

"Um. What does that mean?" she asked.

"Dragons, a phoenix, and more, all coming out in greater numbers than we've seen in many a year." Sage pointed. "See here? This is where the great red dragon lives. I believe it was asleep, or at least far away, for many decades but now is active again. And the trouble it has been causing will only be the beginning, if I'm right. We do *not* want a dragon attacking the villages. That will go very poorly for people."

"And these," he said pointing at Seabrook and the others on the coast, "are where the phoenix has been attacking." He looked at Amber knowingly.

Amber put her hands to her head. "So it *was* a phoenix!"

"Yes. Indeed."

"This is terrible. And you said there's more?"

"Indeed." Sage stroked his wispy beard. "Much, much more. I'm afraid we may be seeing only the beginning."

"Do you know what's causing all of this?" Basil asked.

"Possibly. Possibly . . ." Sage trailed off.

Basil cocked his head to look the wizard in the eyes. "We were thinking it was some sort of magic."

"Yes, of course." Sage whisked his hand in the air. "But the question is, who's behind it?"

Basil looked at the others with eyebrows raised.

"Yes. It is dark magic that has awakened all these creatures. A very powerful spell indeed. Powerful enough to cross hundreds of miles. Most likely there are many behind it, and they have traveled to a number of locations."

Sage looked out the window, lost in thought. "Yes, yes. At least four wizards, I would think. Possibly five. Or three very powerful ones with some help."

Amber was curious about the old man's way of talking—he sometimes spoke directly to them, and other times he appeared lost in his own thoughts, talking to himself. He seemed to go back and forth between the two with ease. But it was somewhat confusing . . . was he talking to the trio . . . or to himself?

Sage looked back at the three kids. "Or . . ." He pointed dramatically. "They have a powerful leader and help from some relics. Yes, that's possible. Indeed. I can think of one or two who would cause quite a bit of trouble of this sort."

"W-w-what," Theo asked, "um . . . what are you thinking to do about it?"

"Do? My dear boy, do?" Sage patted his robes and pulled out a long ornate pipe, which he lit and took a puff. "Why, there is so very much to do! Yes, yes. Indeed. Very much we must do. And soon!" He turned his head to look at Theo with his right eye.

Theo waited silently for the old wizard to continue.

After a moment, Sage went on: "There's a very old prophecy that comes to mind. I have no clue whether it refers to today or if it's about hundreds of years from now, but it involves a great evil taking over our world for much, much too long, and all good folks living in hiding during that time. Unless . . ."

Theo, Amber, and Basil all watched the wizard attentively while he stoked his pipe and continued looking out the window. "If I recall, the prophecy mentions that the evil can be stopped by youngsters who are able to unite the six core elements. In fact . . ." Sage paused and looked at Theo, "I do have to wonder with the powers before me right now if I may have found some of those youngsters."

Theo gulped. "What do you mean? Powers?"

"Yes." Sage stood up. "All three of you possess the capacity for elemental magic."

The three looked at each other curiously.

As if he heard their thoughts, Sage strode over to a bookshelf and continued. "Elemental magic is where a magician can manipulate the world around them without the need for spells, wands, potions, or the like." He pulled a book off the shelf and placed it onto the table, then looked the three of them in the eyes. "All they need is themselves."

He opened the book and leafed through the pages, then pointed at a diagram, and the others drew nearer to see. "This shows the different elemental powers. You can see there are six. Generally speaking, no wizard will have more than one at a time, unless they are special indeed, or they use the power of a wand or scepter."

He pointed at the center. "They are all held together by the ether, which gives power, or mana, to them. Now, I don't have specifics—prophecies are elusive and cryptic at best—but I imagine there will be a way to break the spell by somehow uniting these elements. Of course, those who are involved will need to know how to use their powers."

He stared at them each individually for a moment, then went on. "I have no way of knowing whether any or all of you are the youths referred to in the prophecy, or what your powers are. All I know is that I see mana in all three of you—each of you has a natural gifting in an elemental power."

"The key to unlocking it is to recognize it and explore the boundaries of what you can do with it. So look at this diagram."

Sage pointed at the drawing again and paused. "Over the course of your short years, were there any of these that you felt particularly good at navigating, like you were gifted?"

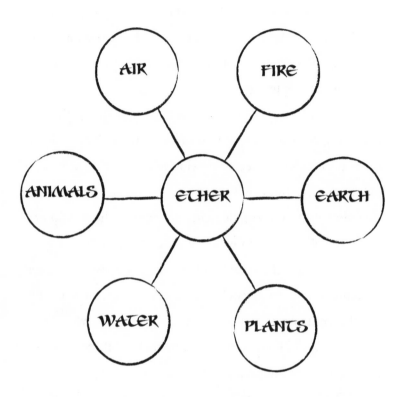

The three stared at the diagram while their minds raced. Basil spoke first. "Theo's always been an animal magnet. Animals love him. What do you think, Theo? Think you've got the elemental power over animals?"

Theo shrugged his shoulders. "I don't know. It never

seemed special to me. Just normal."

Sage nodded. "That's a good sign. Theo, if that is your power, what you need to do is try using it more intentionally. See if you can get into the minds of animals and if you can encourage them to do what you ask."

"All three of you," Sage continued with a sweep of his hand, "have powers and can learn to harness them. You have to figure out what they are and begin using them. The more you use them, the more power you'll find yourself having."

Amber considered the different options. "I live by the sea, so I've always felt comfortable with water. But I've also been great with plants—everyone in Seabrook says I have a green thumb. But what about these others? Maybe I just haven't had the right moment to know I have a gift?"

She glanced at Basil, who shrugged his shoulders. She smiled and shrugged her shoulders as well.

Theo looked confused. "So we'll try to figure out these powers, but what's next? What are *you* going to do?"

"I must find out more about who's casting this spell over the creatures—and from where. I plan to journey across the plains and seek the counsel of some other wizards. And as for you three—however much I'd love to help you learn more about your gifts, you are needed here."

"I don't believe it's a coincidence that the three of you

with elemental powers showed up in my lookout residence when I happened to be here. Whether it's the prophecy or not, these are the kinds of things that don't happen by accident. You will be needed here to slow down the destruction of these creatures."

"How would we do that?" Basil asked. "We're just three kids, and we don't even know what our powers are yet." He turned to Amber and Theo, who nodded emphatically.

"Well, with magic, of course." Sage held his hands out grandly. "You're going to need some way of lifting the spell." He walked over to another book, then began leafing through the pages.

"Let's see. Something you can take with you. A staff? No, too difficult, and you'd need to know how to cast the spell. Let's see. An amulet? Yes, that's it. It can hold enough power in it, and we can put it on a long chain to get it over their heads. It would have to be very long, of course. But that's no problem. The amulet can cancel the spell when it gets around their necks."

Theo cleared his throat. "Um, are you saying you want us to put an amulet around the necks of some goblins? Because that sounds dangerous."

"Oh dear me, no." Sage shook his head. "Goblins are the least of our concern. I'd suggest going straight for the phoenix!"

Amber turned pale and sat down. Theo suddenly felt lightheaded, and Basil choked.

"You think *we* are capable of finding the phoenix and putting an amulet around its neck without getting killed?" Basil asked. "How on earth would we be able to do that?"

Sage smiled. "I'll see what I can whip up."

Chapter 15

Good Gifts

"LET'S SEE," THE OLD WIZARD SAID, rummaging around in a drawer. "We'll need an amulet or pendant."

"I have a pendant." Amber pulled it out from under her shirt.

"Wonderful. Let's have a look." Sage put his hand out, and Amber gave it to him.

Sage's eyes lit up. "Oh, we wouldn't want to enchant *that* one. You hold onto that one."

"Why? What is it?"

"Oh, it's got its own purpose. Where did you get it?"

"It's been in my family a long time."

"Ah. Perfect." Sage nodded and handed it back. "Then it's in the right hands. Keep it well."

"But what is it?" Amber was frustrated. Why did Sage talk like the pixies, so mysteriously?

"Well, it's a wizard's pendant, of course," Sage replied. "It most certainly has some properties or other for the wizard and his or her descendants. Which I'm assuming is you."

"I'm related to a wizard?" Amber was suddenly very confused.

"Of course. Which explains why you'd have an elemental power. It's not a guarantee, mind you. I'm guessing no one else in your family practices magic?"

"No. Not at all. Nobody's even talked about it."

"Well, no matter. I imagine someone or other in your family probably has some gifting. Regardless, try not to lose this pendant. I don't know what it does, but it certainly does something."

"My mom said it brings luck. And my dad said I'm related to someone named Majestic Rose . . ."

"Luck? Interesting." The wizard stroked his beard. "That's a hard spell to create. Very hard indeed. That would explain why Rose was always the most unscathed." He chuckled, then his eyes glossed over and they saw him smile for the first time.

"Well then, time to work." He stood up abruptly and headed to the upstairs chamber. They heard all sorts of clanking noises and Sage talking to himself. The three friends sat quietly, looking at each other.

Amber shook her head, confused. "He talked as if he saw her. My mom said she's like a great-great-great grandmother. Do you think Sage is that old?"

Theo shrugged his shoulders. "Well, he is a wizard. I don't know much about magic. But I would guess he's figured out a way to stay alive longer."

Amber gazed out the window lost in thought.

Basil set down the book with the diagram, went over to a jar of water and stared at it for a while. "I'm not sure what you could do if you had power over water . . . But I don't think I'm doing it."

Theo laughed. "You could drink some. That'll show it!"

Basil and Amber laughed as well. Then Basil lifted his hand and began swirling his fingers around. Amber watched, then turned back to the window, deep in thought.

If I have power over plants, what does that mean? She stared at the trees below. Would I be able to help them grow? She focused on the trees. They seemed like ordinary, everyday trees. Nothing different than any other time she'd paid trees any attention.

She closed her eyes and tried to get a sense of the closest tree in front of her. She waited until she could somewhat sense its presence, then she thought, Okay, tree. Grow. She imagined the tree growing and had a feeling that there was a small disease where a branch had once been. She imagined the disease healing and the tree stretching to the skies.

"Whoa!" Theo stood next to her. "Are you doing that?"

She opened her eyes. The tree was actively growing right in front of her. It was at least four feet taller than before she'd closed her eyes—and it was still growing ever so slowly upward, toward the sky. Her eyes grew wide and she thought, Okay, stop!

The tree stopped growing, and she smiled. "I guess I've figured out my power!"

Theo patted her on the back. "I'd say! That tree looks like the healthiest one around."

She turned to Basil, who was still swirling his hand around. "Figure anything out, Basil?" He shook his head.

Just then, Sage called from upstairs. "A blade! Does anyone use a sword?"

"I do," Basil called back. He walked up the stairs and showed his short sword to the wizard.

"Perfect." The wizard snatched the sword out of his hands and returned to his muttering.

Basil looked confused but walked back down the stairs to his friends. "Well, whatever he's doing with my sword, I hope he doesn't break it. That's my favorite."

Amber and Theo shrugged.

When the wizard finally came down again, it was getting dark. The trio had climbed down to care for their horses and get some food from the saddlebags for dinner. When they got back to the house, Sage was grinning ear to ear.

"We're all set," he said. "They'll be ready by tomorrow."

"What are *they*?" Amber asked.

"Well, the amulet, of course!" Sage said. "That, and a few helpful items I'm sure you'll be able to put to good use. Now there are a few things you should know about enchanted items. First, and most important, you can't use more than a few enchanted items at a time before weakening the effect of all of them, as well as make your own powers more difficult. These are powerful gifts—but be aware if you have other items." He looked at the pendant on Amber's neck. "Keep track of them so that you don't hinder your natural powers."

"Second, enchanted items have a lifespan. I've imbued these with plenty of mana, so they'll all work more than once. But every time they're used, it saps some of the mana, till they're less and less effective and eventually the enchantment is gone. No need to worry with these, though. They'll last at least a year of heavy use with the enchantment I put on them." He looked proudly upstairs, then back to the three.

"Third—and not relevant to you today but perhaps down the road—wands, scepters, and staffs are different. They don't interfere with other enchanted items or your elemental powers. They do require internal mana to cast their spells, so most folks aren't able to use them. Not even all elementalists are able to use them, but many can with practice."

"Scepters only have one purpose, one spell they can cast. And they get more powerful when used in combination with other scepters with multiple wizards using them together. Wands, on the other hand, can do much, much more—but only within their realm. Much like elemental powers, wands stick to one type of spell, like illusions, conjuring, or transmutation. And staffs . . ." Sage looked at the staff in his hand and smiled. "Let's just say they help make enchantments a lot easier."

"What are our items?" Basil asked eagerly. "I know you took my sword."

"Of course. Of course." Sage brushed the air. "You must be patient. No need telling you now. You'll have to wait till morning, when they're ready."

Amber looked up the stairs eagerly. What sort of items

could they be? She was so excited, imagining what sort of magic was being whipped up and what her newfound powers might be able to do that she found it hard to sleep that night. She tossed and turned and didn't feel very rested. But the sun came up earlier than normal on the top of the mountain, and she awoke with the rest of the group at the break of dawn.

After a pleasant breakfast of porridge, Sage stood and brushed off his sleeves. "I think they should be ready by now. Let's go see."

The three could hardly wait. Theo bobbed up and down nervously. When the old man came down the stairs, they eagerly peered at what he was carrying.

"This . . . is the amulet." He held up a pendant a little smaller than Amber's palm, with silver backing and a red stone in the middle, dangling from a particularly long chain. "This should be what's needed to free the phoenix. Put this around the neck of any enchanted creature, and it will break the spell instantly. They'll also be immune to the effects of that particular spell for the rest of their lives."

As Sage handed the amulet to Amber, she examined it more closely. It looked like a fairly average necklace pendant—nothing extravagant or magical.

"This is Basil's sword." Sage held it out with both hands. "I've enchanted it with a few spells. It will have no trouble cutting through any material, even the thickest dragon scales. It also will light up when it's near any creature who's been enchanted by the spell."

Basil took his sword and peered at it curiously from different angles. It appeared no different than before, and he wondered if what the wizard said was even true.

"And now for something very special indeed." Sage held out a hooded cape to Amber. "Take this cape. It has a number of great spells on it, mostly for protection."

She took the cape and looked it over. It was large and brown, designed for a taller person, but she imagined she'd be able to wear it without tripping on it.

"That cape can resist fire and protect its wearer from most regular attacks. And finally," Sage said with a smile, "this ring." He held it up happily. It looked like a simple, silver band, with no unusual markings on it. "The wearer of this ring will have extra protection from harm and also be able to bring quick healing by the laying on of hands."

He held it up to the light, then handed it to Theo. "Wear it at all times," he said sternly. "You never know when trouble is around the corner."

Theo nodded and put it on immediately.

"Can I try it out?" he asked.

Sage nodded.

"Does your arm still hurt, Basil?" Theo asked.

"Yeah. It's stiff and sore. And it's my sword arm too." Basil winced as he moved it.

"Let's see." Theo went over to him and placed the hand wearing the ring on Basil's arm.

"Wow! Amazing!" Basil moved his arm loosely. "It's as if it never happened!"

Sage smiled. "Adventurers get into all sorts of scrapes and bruises. Better to be bold going in, knowing a speedy recovery is only minutes away."

"This is fantastic!" Basil happily swung his sword and lifted his arm.

"I feel great too!" Theo said, standing up straight. "It's like I got a good night's sleep in my own bed last night. Amber, want to see if you could use a little healing?"

"I don't know that I need anything," she shrugged. Theo walked over and put his hands on her. "Wow!" Her face lit up and her eyes brightened. "I didn't realize how achy I was! I feel like I got a great night's sleep!"

Sage was beaming. "I think you'll find the other items just as helpful. Especially the amulet."

Theo interjected, "Seriously? Even with all of these enchanted gifts, do you really think we can get close enough to the phoenix to put the amulet around its neck?"

"That's a good question." Sage stroked his wispy beard thoughtfully. "And I don't have the answer. But one thing is certain. The fact that you three made it all this way from your homes without even knowing you have elemental powers shows me you have the spirit that's needed, and that's far more than the others in this land." He waved his hand toward the window. "But perhaps you could use a little game."

"Game?" All three turned their attention toward the old wizard.

Sage wandered over to a shelf and pulled off a rectangular box. He brushed off the dust and placed it on the table. "This," he said, opening it up to reveal many small pieces and a patterned board, "is a strategy game called Castles."

The youths looked at each other with raised eyebrows. Sage didn't seem particularly crazy, but what good would a game do for all the battles and adventures they were about to face?

Chapter 16

Castles

SAGE PLACED THE PATTERNED BOARD onto the table and dumped the pieces out.

"How does it work?" Theo asked, picking up a piece and examining it.

Sage placed a dragon figurine on a square. "There are two players. The light-colored pieces belong to one player, and the darker to the other. The goal is to maneuver your pieces so that you eliminate enough of the other's pieces to gain the most power on the board."

As he explained the game and each piece, the three friends watched carefully. Each piece had a different movement, and some were weak while others more powerful. Soldiers could only move one space at a time, while the dragons could cross the entire board in one move. He showed them a few examples of different scenarios, and it became clear that every piece could play an important role.

They tried playing the game, and Sage asked them questions on their turn. "Now think ahead. Think more than this move. Think two or three—or even four—moves ahead. What could you do to take over your opponent's most important pieces to claim the power spot?"

Theo was a natural and picked up the game instantly, so Sage focused mostly on helping Amber and Basil as they played against him, game after game until they all got the hang of it.

After playing through lunch and some of the afternoon, Sage declared, "Now it's time. All three of you work together and play against me. When you can beat me in a game of Castles, I'll consider you ready to tackle the phoenix."

"Seriously?" Theo looked pale. "A board game will prepare us for the phoenix? But it's got talons and fire!"

"Of course, of course." Sage patted Theo on the arm. "But the phoenix doesn't have strategy! It's a simple creature, planning only one move ahead. You must learn to think three, four, or even six moves ahead of it."

Theo shook his head. Ridiculous! he thought, but sat down with Basil and Amber across from Sage.

"And so we begin," Sage said. "You may make the first move."

The game began with Theo sitting in the middle seat moving the pieces, and Basil and Amber whispering in his ears. And although they had learned much from playing all that day, they were helpless against Sage's prowess. He won the first game within a few minutes.

"Another game!" Sage said. "You must see more moves ahead. Your view is too short."

Theo gazed at the board curiously. It was kind of like solving a riddle—and he loved riddles. They set up the board again, and Basil sat in the middle seat. His first move was to place a simple soldier piece forward, a strategy that had helped him beat Amber earlier that day.

Sage countered, and Basil quickly began losing pieces. Sage didn't seem concerned in any given moment and always seemed to be able to set up his pieces for winning combinations well in advance of what Basil could come up with.

Sage won within a few minutes. "Again," he said.

The kids shifted seats again, this time Amber took the middle seat. She tried something new. Maybe an approach they hadn't seen yet would help? The game was over in four minutes.

She slumped in her seat, and Sage placed his palms on the table. "Again."

They played over and over throughout the rest of the day. At one point they stopped to make food and check on their horses. While they were out of Sage's earshot, Basil talked quietly to them. "Do you think this is helping? Or is he really just a crazy old man after all?"

"He can't just be a crazy old man." Theo had a renewed sense of energy. "He gave us magical stuff, right? He obviously knows a thing or two."

"Ok." Basil shook his head. "But doesn't this feel like a waste of time? Shouldn't we be getting out there and doing something useful?"

"I don't know." Amber pulled on her hair for a moment. "I don't quite understand why he thinks we need to beat him in Castles, but he's been the best source of any help so far. Just 'cause we don't understand it, doesn't mean it's not useful."

"That's true," Basil said, thoughtfully. "But it's not going to teach us about swordplay or sneaking up on the phoenix or even how to get a chain with an amulet around the neck of it. We should probably be practicing stuff like that as well."

Theo paced and stroked his chin. A gray squirrel scurried out of a tree and sat watching him closely. "He keeps telling us to think four or more moves ahead, but I think he sees more like *ten* moves ahead! If we're going to beat him, we need to try something different."

"Like what?" Amber asked.

"I don't know yet, but we need to come up with something."

"Wait, I have an idea." Basil held out his hands grandly. "What if we make a move that *looks* bad, but not too bad, and then he thinks we've made a simple mistake and falls into a trap!"

"Interesting." Theo nodded. "Yes, we could try to draw him in by tricking him. But how?"

The three discussed it and drew strategies in the dirt with sticks and used rocks and acorns for the pieces. They considered a number of different ways to win.

Theo looked at their makeshift board and stopped Basil from moving a piece. "Wait. Look here. What if we opened up our strongest knight with the weakest soldier?" Theo moved a small rock aside. "And he'd think it's worth coming in to take out our strongest knight, and even give him a chance to win in three moves. But look, I have my cavalryman here, ready to come into the opening he left behind, see? He thinks he's winning, but we'd actually end up with the upper hand."

"Interesting." Basil studied the board more. "Yes, that would definitely have worked against me. But against Sage?"

"I don't know," Theo replied. "It's an idea."

"And a good one," Amber said. "So let's come up with more of them. Not just one."

The boys nodded, and the trio continued to strategize with different scenarios. At one point, Amber elbowed Theo and pointed up. Theo turned to see Sage watching them with a grin on his face. They waved and used their backs to block his view of their rough board.

As it grew dark, the kids climbed back up the ladder. The wizard was reading a book by the window and looked up. "Wonderful. You're back. Another game this evening?"

"Let's do it," Basil said confidently. He sat in the middle and played carefully to set up one of the scenarios they'd come up with. At one point, he made the pretend "flawed" move, where Sage would come in and make his fatal mistake. In fact, Sage picked up the cavalryman as they'd hoped and very nearly took out their knight, but then he smiled and looked at the children.

"Ah. Well done. Well done, indeed. I see you've learned a thing or two today." Sage placed the piece back where it had been and moved his soldier. Basil watched sadly as he proceeded to be trounced by the wizard—yet again.

"Again," Sage said.

This time Amber tried. Her plan was more complicated, and she nearly tricked Sage into making the move she wanted, but he saw through it and won in the end. On Theo's turn, the game became fierce. Both players seemed to have the upper hand at different times. At one point, Theo very nearly won, at least that's how it appeared to the kids. But Sage once again saw the opportunities they hadn't and won.

It was dark outside, and Amber yawned. Sage glanced at her. "We'll pick this up in the morning." He stood and walked up the stairs to the upper chamber.

"You almost had him," Basil said to Theo. "I think we're super close."

"Yeah, but we're missing something. It's like our strategy was good—but not enough. There's got to be something else."

Amber's eyes were drooping. "Did you notice he often won by using his soldiers three moves before his victory?"

"What?" Theo looked at Amber, startled.

"Yeah. Not every game. But moving his soldier was usually what he did three moves ahead of winning."

"Interesting." Theo stared at the board intently.

"I'm going to sleep." Amber staggered over and lay down on the fur near the fireplace.

"Me too." Basil stood up and lay down on another fur.

But Theo stayed up, looking at the board. He played a light-colored piece, then turned the board sideways, turned it again, and turned it again. He played a dark-colored piece and looked at it from the different angles. Then he played another piece from the light-colored side.

He played against himself for hours, with an oil lamp lighting his game. His eyes strained, and he felt exhausted but kept at it. At one point he was so frustrated, he slammed his fist onto the table and walked around. Then he came back and tried again. Maybe a different approach? A different strategy completely? What if he switched strategies partway through?

The room began to brighten, and Theo looked around in surprise. He'd stayed up the entire night. Yet he still didn't have any breakthrough moments where he knew he could win against Sage. He went over to the bucket of water and splashed some on his face. He was missing something, but what?

He returned to the board and continued to play by himself until Amber and Basil woke up.

Basil stretched and looked at Theo. "Have you been up all night?"

Theo nodded silently, peering at the pieces, squinting as if that would somehow help him view the board differently.

"Any new ideas?" Basil stood up and looked at the game board curiously.

"Many," Theo said. "Many new ideas. Yes."

"Great!" Basil grinned, then frowned when Theo looked at the board seriously. "No good ones?"

"Oh, I had many good ideas." Theo rubbed his eyes and fingered one of the cavalrymen. "Yes, I have a dozen new tactics and possible strategies. I've even thought a lot about how Sage has kept winning, and I have some ideas about that as well—both to use his tactics as well as to prevent them. But will it be enough to beat him? I . . . I just don't know."

Basil smiled again and patted Theo on the back. "If any of us can do this, it's you, Theo. Come on, take a break. Let's get some air and make some breakfast."

As if on cue, Theo's stomach growled. He looked up at Basil and smiled weakly. "You're right. I could use a break."

They climbed down the ladder and checked on their horses. Basil nudged Theo. "Come on, Butterballs. You always pull through with this kind of stuff. Relax for once."

Theo looked at him annoyed for a moment, then

relaxed, his thoughts starting to come together. Basil can be annoying, but he's right. It won't help to be anxious about it. It's supposed to be a game, right? He felt himself smiling. "Ok, Squiggles. I'll try to relax. Maybe I should take a little nap."

"Yeah. We want you to be sharp before you sit down in front of the wizard."

A nap did Theo some good, and he awoke to the smell of warm porridge and gentle talk. Amber was peering through the telescope again, while Basil and Sage sat at the table, discussing elemental powers.

"You see," Sage was saying, "once you learn your power, you'll have to practice. Just like using that sword of yours. The first time you use it, you can certainly cut things with it, but it takes years of practice to use it well in battle."

"Of course. But I still don't know my power. Are you sure I have one?"

"Oh yes. Definitely. Keep exploring. It'll all become obvious once you figure it out."

Theo rubbed his eyes and joined them at the table. Sage looked at him with a twinkle in his eyes, as if he knew what Theo was up to all night.

After breakfast, when the table was cleared, Sage set the game down again. "Are you ready for another round?"

Basil patted Theo on the back and Amber smiled at him. Theo nodded seriously and sat down in the middle seat across from Sage. As they set up the board, he said. "Sage, I'd like to offer you to go first this time."

Sage raised his eyebrows. "Awfully generous of you, lad. Are you sure? You might be playing defense the entire game."

"Let's give it a try."

Sage nodded and made the first move. Theo quickly countered with a move of his own, and the game was on. For every move Sage made, Theo moved his piece quickly and with confidence, as if he'd already thought through what he was going to do. Sage, on the other hand, took his time thinking through every move carefully.

Much like the games they'd played the night before, they both took out each other's pieces, and the board became sparse. Sage made a bold move, and Theo finally paused, then smiled. Instead of taking out Sage's piece, he did a move that seemed purely defensive and weak.

Amber was puzzled, but then noticed Sage frown. She looked more closely, trying to see more than two moves into the future. It was at move five that she suddenly saw it. Unless she was missing something, Theo was going to win. She held her breath and waited.

Sage paused, then smiled and moved the only option he had. Theo smiled as well, and they both made the next moves quickly, ending with Theo as the victor.

"Well done," Sage said. "Well done. You are ready." He stood and walked to a counter, picking up a leather strap and returned to the table. He put all the pieces into one half of the board and folded it, then tied the leather strap around it.

"Please take this with you as my final gift. When in doubt of what to do next, play Castles again and remember what you've learned. All of you have gained a great deal of new insight in this last day. Don't diminish the power of a game to teach you something important."

"If the evil magicians behind these occurrences are truly who I think they are, then they have thought many, many moves in advance of us. They've plotted this longer than you kids have been alive."

He paused, and all were silent for a moment. Finally Amber spoke. "Thank you, Sage. For all you've done."

He nodded. "I've given you what I can. I may be gone for a while. I have many unanswered questions. Focus on the phoenix first. And slow down or stop any enchanted creatures in general. Save as many people from harm as you can. And who knows," Sage said wryly, "perhaps some of the creatures who get freed from the spell might want to help."

Chapter 17

The Dark

ACCORDING TO SAGE, the phoenix lived in a somewhat-active volcano four mountains over, northeast, by the sea. When they had looked through the telescope to see how they might get there, they saw no clear roads that went that way, but they found a route on the next mountain that seemed to have less trees.

Theo updated his map and drew a little picture of a phoenix on the volcano, with smoke coming out of the mountaintop.

"Nice drawing!" Amber said, looking over his shoulder. "You have a gift."

"Thanks. It's always been a hobby of mine." Theo grinned and rolled the map up. "Time to get moving."

Their journey down the mountain was slower than they would have liked, since the trees were so close together and there was underbrush everywhere. They meandered down a winding path used by deer and other wildlife. At one point, a large branch completely blocked their path. The underbrush was so dense that their horses would have had difficulty getting around.

Amber fixed her eyes on the branch and sensed its life force, then asked it to move. It slowly bent itself back away from the path. She lifted her hands instinctively and moved them in the direction she wanted it to go, which caused it to move faster.

Theo clapped his hands. "Way to go!"

She gritted her teeth and continued moving the branch till it was completely away from the path.

"That's a nice little trick." Basil sat upright in his saddle with his fists on his hips. "Keep it up!"

They continued, pausing every once in a while for her to move branches out of the way. Every time she used her powers, she grew a little more tired—so after a while she took a break and they moved around the branches the old-fashioned way or hacked at them with swords.

As they neared the base of the mountain, Basil suddenly stopped and raised his hand. "Quiet!"

Amber and Theo stopped their horses and listened. Basil took his sword out of its sheath and looked at it curiously. It was glowing a light orange color.

To their left they heard some muffled voices speaking in a guttural language. Amber quietly pulled her bow off and notched an arrow. Theo got a strange look of concentration in his eyes.

Suddenly, a brown hawk came flying low from behind them, circled Theo once, then flew toward the sounds.

"I think there are four of them. No wait, five." Theo's eyes glazed over, focused on something out of sight. "Definitely goblins. They're walking through the woods. Heading away. I think we should just stay put."

The goblin voices continued moving faintly into the distance, and Basil's sword dimmed and finally went out. He held it out with a flourish. "Well, *that's* pretty useful!"

Amber slung her bow on her back and sighed in relief. "That's great, Basil! And, Theo, what did you do with that hawk? Can you actually see what it sees?"

"Well, not exactly. It's not like I'm seeing through the hawk's eyes. But I do get a sense of things—like what its reaction is to the things around it. I wasn't controlling the hawk. I don't know that I can actually do that . . . more like I can give it ideas. If it's open to them."

"Your powers seem to be the furthest along." Basil sheathed his sword. "Can you keep that hawk around for a while, to keep a lookout for us?"

"I suppose I can ask it to. Yes." Theo focused on the hawk again, and it did a loop around him before flying above the treetops.

They continued on their way and soon left the dense trees behind for shrubs, grass, and rocky terrain. With less trees, the next mountain had more routes, and Basil soon found a good, clear path. There were a few crumbly spots, but all in all, it was a fairly easy journey on their horses. They didn't go straight up, which would have been too steep, but crossed back and forth, up and around the mountain.

The air felt crisp and fresh, and Amber wondered if they were near the sea yet. Theo tried asking the hawk to do some loops in the air and then land on his shoulder. The hawk obliged.

"Pretty amazing stuff, Theo," Basil said admiringly. "Hey, see if you can get it to hunt for us. We could use some fresh rabbit."

"Good idea!" Theo closed his eyes for a moment and the hawk flew off. Every once in a while, it would swoop down, then circle back to Theo. After an hour, it came back with a rabbit clenched in its claws.

"Look at that! It worked!" Basil grinned. The hawk flew to Theo and released the rabbit into his hands. Theo mentally thanked it and asked it to continue to circle and keep looking. The hawk once again obliged and flew above them.

As the sun dipped low in the sky, they started looking for a place to camp. They rounded a rocky bend and came across a cave. In front of it was a wide area with lush grasses, some protective trees, and good views of the area.

Basil dismounted and scanned the surrounding ground. "This seems like a decent spot. We could stay in the cave if the weather turns on us, and this area is mostly level. A perfect place to camp!"

Amber and Theo agreed and dismounted. They unloaded their food and camping gear from their horses and tied them to a nearby tree. As they began thinking of dinner, the hawk returned with another small rabbit.

Basil started making a fire. "Hooray! More fresh food! It's enough for all of us, even the hawk. Let's cook it up!"

Soon they were enjoying a warm fire and the freshly cooked rabbit. Theo thanked the hawk and gave it some food. He asked it to return in the morning; he sensed it was agreeable to that.

As they sat around the fire, Basil took another bite of rabbit and relaxed. "So, Theo, what's it like having influence over animals?"

"It feels really normal, actually." Theo looked into the dark forest, thinking. "I guess I've always done it, but I didn't know it. Animals have always come to me, and I feel a connection with them. I never tried asking them what to do, though."

"Yeah, that's pretty cool . . . what you did today with that hawk."

"For sure." Theo took a bite. "What about you? Have you figured anything out yet?"

"It's hard to say." Basil held his hand up and twisted it around. "I wonder if I'm doing something, but I can't tell. When I twirl my hand around like this, I feel like I'm moving the air, but then I guess that's pretty normal, right? I don't think I'm making it blow harder or anything crazy."

"Huh. Don't know." Theo shook his head. "There's also fire. Try seeing if you can do something with the campfire."

Basil stared at the fire for a while. He waved his hand and the flames grew higher.

"Yeah, that's it, Basil! Keep trying."

Basil moved his hand again and watched the fire move with him. "I don't know. Maybe it's fire, and maybe it's air."

He twirled his hands again, watching the flame dance in the same swirling motion he did. He was definitely doing something.

Amber watched, then grew tired and thought of her own powers. She closed her eyes and felt the forest around her. It seemed like she could tell more about what was where. She was even beginning to tell the difference between the types of trees.

Not that she knew what the different kinds of trees were called, but she could tell when one was tall with wide leaves and when one was short, wispy, and blew in the wind. She wondered how far she could sense the different plants.

Deep down she pictured the forest surrounding them, dense trees and vegetation in every direction. She pushed the feeling, and was able to sense farther and farther away. Eventually, the feeling dimmed, and she couldn't sense any more, about a stone's throw away.

She kept her eyes closed and focused on a nearby tree, trying to see if she could make its branch grow toward her. She opened her eyes. It was dark out and getting harder to see, but the branch had indeed grown in her direction, as she'd imagined. She thought about it having little twigs pop out of the side, and it did. Then she thought to have the branch do a little spiral, and it did.

But it wasn't easy. Every time she encouraged the trees and plants to do things for her, she felt some of her energy drain. After a full day of trying out her powers, she wasn't sure how much more she could do.

Theo interrupted her thoughts. "Anyone for a game of Castles?"

"Sure," Basil replied. "But go easy on me! Maybe you can show me how you beat Sage."

"Sounds good." Theo pulled the game out.

Amber sighed. "Well, boys, I'm pooped. Good night."

"Good night," they said in unison.

✳ ✳ ✳

Amber slept instantly and deeply. In her dreams, she walked out into the forest, and the trees began talking to her.

"You've finally started to listen, Amber."

"Well, I didn't realize I wasn't listening before," Amber replied.

"Yes, but now you're actually listening. Before you were barely there. We have so much to tell you."

"Like what?"

"We trees know a great many things. We've been around a long time, you know."

"Really? Like, you in particular?"

"No, no. But we live a long time. You people can live forty, fifty, maybe even a hundred years. We trees can live a thousand."

"Really? And do all of you talk like this?"

"No. But many of us do. To people like you. We always have. We want to tell you so many things, Amber."

"Like what?"

"We want you to know what it looks like when the land is at peace. When the trees are at peace. We can all live together, you know. The elves do that. You humans could learn a thing or two from them."

Amber was intrigued. She knew, somehow, that she was dreaming, yet wondered if this was a real conversation. "What sorts of things do the elves do with the trees that we humans could do better?"

"Well, for one, you could work with us, rather than chopping us down all the time for your homes."

"How would we do that—work with you?" Amber asked.

"Through people like you."

"Ah. Of course." Amber paused.

"And there's something else you should know. It's not just us trees that have important things to tell you."

"Really?" Amber replied. "What else?"

"Remember to always pay attention to your horses."

Amber listened. The horses were neighing and unhappy. She awoke with a start.

The fire had nearly gone out, and the others were sleeping. The moon had passed over, so it was particularly dark. Amber squinted toward the horses who were clearly upset. Her ears pricked when she realized there was a large, but quiet, creature coming toward them through the trees.

"Basil! Theo!" Amber whispered loudly. "Wake up! There's something out there."

Basil and Theo stirred awake, and Amber pointed. Basil quietly unsheathed his sword, which glowed a bright orange. The three of them rolled out of their beds. Amber took her bow, even though she could barely see a thing in the dark. Theo and Basil held their swords.

They waited in the dark, hearts pounding. Amber kept watching the woods, then caught her breath and whispered again, "There are creatures out there. They're very large."

The three edged closer together, when suddenly a huge troll leaped from the trees into the clearing, holding up a large club.

In the dim moonlight, its body appeared to be made of stone, with random formations all over its arms and back, almost like calcified rock growths. Its head was gruesome—a tiny nose, humongous mouth with fangs, and evil squinty eyes. There wasn't an ounce of fat anywhere to be seen . . . a creature of muscle, stone, and power.

Amber let loose an arrow straight into its body. It penetrated the chest, but the arrow looked like a little pin prick in the enormous body. The troll clomped toward Basil and swung his club, an enormous wooden, spiky weapon.

The troll was so slow compared to Basil that he easily dodged to the side of the creature and leaped in, thrusting his enchanted short sword into its side, leaving a noticeable gash.

Basil jumped to the troll's back side and thrust his sword again, before the creature whirled around, swinging its dangerous club directly at him. Basil rolled clear, far from the troll, scraped by some rocks and breathing heavily.

Meanwhile, a second troll came crashing through the trees into the clearing, wielding a similar spiky club. Amber fired arrow after arrow into the first troll, with seemingly no effect.

Basil jumped in and stabbed the second troll with his sword, penetrating the thick hide and causing the troll to grunt. Then Basil jumped back, fell over a tree root and rolled away.

With the second troll distracted by Basil's attack, Theo stabbed at it, but his sword bounced off, leaving only a tiny nick. He ran away yelling, "My sword's useless against them!"

Amber shot another arrow into the first troll, down to her last three. The arrow looked like a little twig on the troll's massive body. "Basil, we need to get out of here!" she yelled.

"The cave!" Basil ran toward it at full speed. Amber and Theo quickly tore out, following him. The trolls clambered after them as the trio neared the cave entrance. One of them swung its enormous club and they felt the wind rushing just behind them. Too close for comfort. One blow would mean certain death.

The cave entrance was large, even for the trolls, and Amber had an awful thought: Is this their home? Are we running into our death? There was no time to change their minds. Basil's glowing sword led the way into the cave and down a forked tunnel. He took a left turn, Amber and Theo still following him, as the sound of trolls crashing against the cave echoed loudly behind them.

"Ow!" Theo yelled after stubbing his toe badly, but he continued limping behind Amber and Basil.

The tunnel wound and narrowed, then opened again to a wider section with stalagmites all across the cave floor, requiring the kids to slow down so they wouldn't accidentally impale themselves.

Basil's sword continued to glow brightly, giving them

enough light to see the piercing rocks. And also telling them they were far from safe. They made it through—but the trolls continued to close in. The sound of their large stomping feet and bulging bodies scraping on tight walls resounded in the larger room.

"This way!" Basil called, turning toward a tunnel that he hoped would be too small for the enormous creatures.

They continued to run and scramble over rocks and down tunnels as they split in various directions, taking them further into the cave. The passageway narrowed slightly, but the trolls were still clearly on their tail.

"Going into a cave was the wrong way to get away from trolls!" Theo moaned as he banged his knee on a stalagmite. "They're so fast here, even with their size."

"Well it's too late now, isn't it?" Basil's eyes flashed angrily.

"Look!" Amber said. "A small passageway over on the left. Come on!" They veered into a smaller channel that the trolls would definitely not fit through.

"Let's hope this isn't a dead end!" Theo complained. "It looks like it might not go all the way through."

But thankfully, the narrow channel didn't seem to have an immediate end, and after a few minutes, the glow in Basil's sword began to dim. Finally, it was so dim they couldn't see the full passage in front of them, and they stopped.

They stood in silence, hearts pounding. The sound of their ragged breathing became somehow comforting. The area became completely still. They had survived an impossible encounter.

Theo was the first to speak. "I'm thankful to be alive. And I think we lost the trolls. But . . . I think we're also lost."

Amber and Basil stood quietly as the realization sunk in. They were alive, but all their belongings and their horses were out there with the trolls. They were in a huge cave system with many different passageways, no light source, and no idea which way they'd come.

Basil's sword glowed more faintly until the light completely disappeared. The three were swallowed by complete and utter darkness.

Chapter 18
Goblin Army

THE CAVERNOUS ROOM was eerily quiet as Lucio strode confidently through the giant doors to the throne room of the goblin king—an overweight hobgoblin, twice the size of the smaller goblins and hobgoblins standing around him.

He sat on an ornate throne holding a bronze scepter with ten small gems on the tip. He was as ugly as any goblin, with an enormous warty nose, flabby green cheeks, and wide, pointy ears. A golden crown, embedded with precious gems around its circumference, rested on his head.

Dozens of goblins and hobgoblins lined the walls of the echoey room, watching the human carefully with their weapons at the ready. Torches burned all along the walls, flickering dimly in the large chamber.

"Your highness," the dark wizard said smoothly. "How are your preparations going?"

"Bah!" The giant goblin snorted. He spoke the human tongue sloppily, sounding as if his mouth were full of marbles. "Goblin army best ever. But not what you want. Not so many."

"Indeed. How many will you have gathered in the next month?"

"My kingdom . . . two thousand, including hobgoblins."

"We may need more than that. Have you talked to the other goblin kingdoms?"

"Ha! Ha! Ha!" Spittle formed on the giant goblin's lips. "Us goblins not all get along, you know."

"You really think two thousand will be the most powerful army in history? Maybe you goblins aren't enough?"

"What?" The giant green king stood and slapped his scepter in his other hand. "How dare you speak to me that way! Our army the greatest in entire land!"

"Of course it is." Lucio eyed the scepter in the goblin's hands and his right hand gently rested on the scepter at his own side. "Yours is the largest force around. But perhaps others might join? The other goblins across the land would benefit from working with a king as great as you. And I hear there are some giants in the south lands who could be useful."

"Giants?" The goblin spat on the ground, and the goblins around him tensed. "Goblins *never* work with giants."

Lucio turned to gesture to the other goblins around the room. "This army you've gathered . . . What if you were to encounter a powerful wizard?" With his back turned to the king, he snuck his scepter off his side and lifted it ever so slightly. The purple gem on the tip glowed, and he swirled slowly, pointing it all around the room. All the goblins instantly calmed down, including the king.

"As I was saying, you will appreciate the giants as allies. Never before has the goblin army been so powerful."

"Yes, of course." The king sat down, looking satisfied. "Most powerful goblin army ever!" He grinned and laughed. "With giants, we crush any resistance." He squeezed his beefy hand as if squishing fruit.

"And giants are the start," Lucio continued, keeping the scepter raised. "We will search for other help as well. No power will be able to stand in our way."

"Excellent!" The plump goblin clapped his hands together.

"When do you think the army will be ready?"

"Soon. Soon. Much, much still to prepare. Shelter is needed, to be in the day longer. And more weapons."

"And other goblin kingdoms?"

"Yes. Yes. I send my goblins—go speak to them. They join for victory!"

"Indeed." Lucio thought for a moment. "If it pleases your highness, I'd like to talk with them as well. To tell them how great you are and to come join your forces here."

"Yes. Yes. You talk too. Show how great our army is with giants."

"Wonderful. Your majesty." The wizard bowed slightly and placed the scepter back into its holster, then turned and walked out of the room. Three goblins immediately followed behind him. He strode under goblin escort through winding tunnels until he came to two large doors that were open, revealing daylight.

The goblins shrunk back from the outside light, and Lucio strode through into the open air. The hippogriff stood quietly, waiting for him. He mounted it smoothly, then the creature spread its wings and glided down the mountain and out over the plains.

Dozens of large canopies were set up with hundreds of goblins gathered under them building war catapults. He flew low and circled the area. Below, taller hobgoblins were ordering the shorter goblins who cut down trees, trimmed, sized, and assembled them. The catapults weren't the greatest workmanship Lucio had ever seen, but he smiled slyly. It would be a month, maybe two at the most, before the army would be ready. And by then, it would be the most powerful force on the planet.

The hippogriff soared past the goblins toward another mountain capped in snow. As Lucio drew closer to the mountain, he noticed gargoyles perched in the shade of the largest trees watching him carefully. Their dark, stony hides were hard to spot in the darkness of the enormous redwood branches, but Lucio knew exactly where to look.

After passing the thick forest, he flew toward a perfectly built white-stone castle with six thin spires angling into the sky, partway up the base of the tall mountain. Each was topped with a deep-red pointed roof. Its tall wall was surrounded with turrets and watchful eyes from dozens of different creatures, from bat-like gargoyles to humans and elves.

He coasted over the wall and landed in the wide inner courtyard. As he dismounted, a short elf with green skin and long pointed ears came running out of a building toward him and stood patiently. Lucio strode toward the nearest building and spoke gruffly. "Is Caster back yet?"

"Yes, master." The elf bowed and followed behind quickly. "He is in the planning room."

Lucio barreled past servants at work, cleaning and carrying items. Upstairs he strode into a room with four people in it, including Caster.

Caster's red cape ruffled as he turned to see Lucio. "Ah! Welcome back. I have good news."

Lucio frowned and looked impatient, so Caster quickly continued, "I found two dozen imps who have killed at least as many pixies. They're on the move and heading southwest down the coast. But we need more fires in the next towns—only those who've had fires are leaving their homes."

"Just as I suspected." Lucio folded his arms. "The pixies are resourceful, but most of their power comes from the magic they've put into their homes. When they're on the move, they're far more vulnerable."

He tapped his fingers together. "Check on the imps regularly. We need to keep pressure on the pixies. And don't lose them this time. I don't care if you have to kill all but one. Make sure at least one survives to lead us to that tower of theirs."

"Consider it done." Caster nodded and tapped on some drawings on the table. "And the phoenix?"

"Yes. Yes." Lucio looked annoyed. "I'll pay it another visit. We'll burn the whole coastline if we have to. We're going to find that tower."

"I'll head to the coast as soon as I'm done here." Caster calmly gestured to the three others in the room.

Lucio grunted in reply. He ran his finger down the scepter's shaft, then turned and walked out of the room. When he left, the whole room relaxed. But his words resonated in the air.

The coast wouldn't be safe anymore. Not for a long time.

Chapter 19
Underground

BASIL HAD EXPERIENCED PITCH-DARK BEFORE. But dark at night always had the stars or the moon or the lights from town. Even when he'd camped in the darkness of a thick forest, there was always some light. But this. He looked around the cave in dismay.

There was one time he remembered camping in the deep woods with the moon completely gone and full cloud cover. It'd been so dark that he couldn't see a thing, similar to this. Yet, back then he knew that things would soon change—the sun would return in the morning.

This time was different.

And all three of them realized the same thing: morning wouldn't bring light in the cave. There was no way to know day or night. No way to know left or right. Any hope of escape by the way they'd come, which would already have been a near-impossible task, was fully impossible without light. It was a timeless, directionless darkness. And it overcame any idea of hope.

He heard Amber slump down on the tunnel floor and give out a little whimper. He put his hand out. The cave wall was cold and damp. He felt deep fear settle into his bones. Battling the trolls, however futile, was at least battling enemies in front of them. This was a different kind of scary— an utter sense of being lost more fully than ever, and no idea what to do about it.

He took a deep breath and closed his eyes. When he opened them and looked around, he thought he was seeing flashing lights and stars, like when he would close his eyes tightly. He took another deep breath. "Any ideas now?"

The sound of Theo scuffling and sitting down next to Amber echoed in the silence. "Is one of the elemental powers light?" he asked nervously.

Amber gave a weak chuckle. "No, but that sure would be helpful." They sat in silence for a few moments.

Basil finally spoke. "I have no idea how we'll get out of

here, but using elemental powers sounds like a good thing right now."

"Hey," Theo said. "Basil, the way you controlled the fire earlier . . . what if your power is over air? Maybe you can do something with that?"

"I'll try." Basil moved his hands in circles and felt something, much like the last time, as if he was swirling the air around. That isn't a power, is it? Isn't that normal? He almost stopped, but then with desperation remembered the fire he'd caused to grow. There's got to be something to this, he thought. I need to figure it out. We can't be stuck here forever.

Theo and Amber stayed quiet as he waved his hands around. Little twists of his hands with focus seemed to make the air breeze by. Bigger motions caused it to blow farther and faster. He stopped to feel the air for a moment—a breeze that continued in the direction he last waved, then it died down completely and was still.

The sound of Amber and Theo breathing deeply in sleep filled the cavern.

In the pitch dark, Basil got lost in his thoughts. I can feel the air around me when I move my hands. Maybe I can use that to feel the shape of the tunnel. Basil concentrated on the air around him. Nothing. He tried again, with more focus.

The longer he stood in silence zeroed in on the space around him, the more he felt the dankness and stale quality of the air. But not the shape of the tunnel.

He waved his hand while keeping focused. Instantly the air moved around him from one direction of the tunnel to the other. He could tell that the tunnel stayed consistent in both directions.

He tried again. Yes, he was controlling the air! The difference was subtle. Before he was trying to do it more with his mind and his arms, but there was a deeper power within him that he felt stirring as he practiced. Is that the mana that Sage talked about? Do I just have to figure out how to tap into that, instead of my brain?

He tried again—this time using his mind and arms less and drawing from that deeper source within him to make the air blow. It blew stronger than before, and the shape of the tunnel became clearer. He grew excited. I think I can use this to walk forward without bumping into things!

He blurted out, "I've got it!"

Amber and Theo startled awake.

"Got what?" Theo asked groggily.

"I've figured out how to feel the tunnel. My power is definitely air. I can create wind currents and feel the shape of the tunnel when I do."

"Really?" Theo scuffled around and stood. "So your power is air after all!"

"Yeah," Basil said. "I'm sure of it now. I think we should keep going the same way we were. I think the tunnel goes a long way."

"Ok." Theo was still groggy.

"Let's go then."

"Wait, guys." Amber staggered over and grabbed Basil's arm. "Something weird is going on."

"What is it?" Theo said, concerned.

"I feel like I can sort of see you."

"What do you mean?"

"It's weird. I don't know if it's my imagination, but I see you two, super faint. It's like I see your heat."

"Really?" Basil held her out at arm's length, trying to see her. All he saw was complete darkness. He may as well have had his eyes shut. "Does that have anything to do with your elemental power?"

"I don't think so. How would that be connected with plants? It's odd, like I can see you better when I'm not working at it."

Theo perked up. "Can you see anything else?"

"No. I guess not," Amber replied. "I guess it doesn't help us get out of here."

"No," Basil said. "But I think I can. I feel the air—I can tell which way it's going. I guess air does have a bit of usefulness. Makes me wonder what else I take for granted. Like you two, all this time you didn't know you had powers, you just took it for granted. Maybe I've always had that with the way I can feel the air around me."

He paused. "I can tell where you two are without hearing you. I feel how the wind gets stopped by you, as it's coming through." He reached out and took Amber's hand.

Amber squeezed it. "That's a strong breeze you're creating. It feels nice."

"Yeah, I'm doing that!" Basil squeezed her hand back. "I don't know why it took me so long. It seems so natural now." He took Theo's hand. "Here, Theo, take Amber's other hand. I'll lead the way."

Amber saw the faint heat coming from Theo and reached for his hand. "Ok, we're all linked."

Basil took a faltering step, feeling with his foot and free hand cautiously before moving. It was slow going, and he sensed the need to stop occasionally to refocus.

One slow step after one slow step, they made their way down the tunnel. Even with Basil feeling the air, it was still disconcerting to not see what was in front of them. What if they walked straight into a stalactite? Or fell down a cliff?

After an hour of slow walking, they came to a fork in the passage, and Basil paused. "I feel air currents from two directions."

Amber frowned. "What do you think? Is one better than the other? Or maybe either direction could work?"

"Wait," Theo said. "I think there are some bats ahead to our right." He stood still for a moment, tracking them. "Yes. Bats. There are dozens of them. I'll see if I can get a sense from them if that way leads out." He paused, then sighed. "Of course it leads out—for bats. I don't think they have a sense of how big the passageway needs to be for humans."

They stood in silence for a while, then Basil said, "I need both my hands." He lifted his arms like an orchestra conductor, waving them slightly and drawing from the inner strength that he felt more and more clearly.

Wind gently breezed down the passageway and refreshed the kids' faces. It felt crisp, much different than the rest of the air in the stuffy cave.

"I can feel the currents. To the right is a large passageway. Large enough for all of us, I'm pretty sure. Come on!" Basil took Amber's hand again, and they started walking more quickly toward the right.

Basil never sped to a fast pace, but he was steady and moving more boldly than before.

"Hey, the bats are just up ahead," Theo said.

"I can see them!" Amber grew excited. "They're glowing red, very faintly. There are at least a hundred of them all sleeping on the ceiling."

"That's right," Theo responded. "I sense them too."

Under other circumstances, the bats may have seemed scarier, but in this case, the friends were relieved. It meant they were near the open air.

Basil charged ahead. "It's this way. The outside air is getting stronger." He led them through a passage, then stopped abruptly and felt with his hand. "Okay. Duck your heads here—it's a lower ceiling."

They all crouched as they entered a narrow channel and then started to climb a steeper passage. "We're almost there!" Basil called. "I think we can let go of our hands now. Duck even lower here. Almost at crawling height. Try not to bump your head."

The three crouched and crawled after Basil. "It bends to the left here," he called back. "Ah! Stars!"

The night sky greeted the three like a happy reunion with lost relatives. They simultaneously breathed sighs of relief and scrambled their way up the last rocks till they finally stood in the cool night outside.

Compared to the pitch darkness of the cave, the trio felt like they could see everything. Large and small rocks covered the entire terrain. It was a far different spot than where they'd camped.

Basil drew his sword slightly from its scabbard, but when he saw it wasn't glowing at all, he put it back. "Safe for now."

He sat on a rock and took a deep breath. "That was amazing. I can control air currents!"

Theo patted Basil's back as he sat next to him on the rock, "Awesome. Looks like we've all figured out our powers—and it's only been the first few days on our own. Think of what more we'll discover if we can survive long enough!"

Amber laughed. "Yeah. With all these trolls and creatures, who knows?"

"One thing's for sure." Theo grinned. "*Three* kids with powers sure beats *one!*"

Basil breathed deeply, feeling the air around him. For the first time in his life, he realized what he should have known all along. The air felt like a living, breathing thing. It had a soul. He could tell where the high-pressure spots were pushing the lows and where the cold air was forcing up the warm. It was never still, always moving around joyfully. He joined in, focusing on the air next to him and constricting it. As soon as it became high pressure, it pushed the other air around it.

Curious, he tightened the air even more, and a small cloud began to form. Can I even control the weather? Basil beamed. "It sure is nice to finally know what my power is."

Amber's eyes drooped. "That's great, but now what? I don't want to sleep out here on the rocks, but I'm exhausted."

They considered their surroundings. Up the mountain seemed rocky and unappealing, whereas below were trees and vegetation. They scrambled down some rocks till they came to the trees. They walked a short distance, winding through trees and past bushes. Amber tried to sense the different kinds of vegetation, looking for a bed of grass that would fit all three of them.

"This way," she said, leading them along a path made by forest animals toward a flatter, more welcoming spot. They huddled together and fell asleep instantly.

✶ ✶ ✶

The sun peeked over the ridge of the mountain only an hour later, but the three slept through the sunrise, exhausted from the night's adventure. When they finally awoke, it was to a warm and friendly day. Birds were singing in the nearby trees.

Basil awoke first. He was lying in a tumble with Theo and Amber and felt achy and sore. He rose and stretched, then walked up the trail back to the rocks for a better look. The views were spectacular, but unfamiliar.

One thing he'd learned growing up in similar terrain was to always be aware of your surroundings. He'd paid attention to the shape of mountain peaks and landmarks on trails. There were a dozen ways to figure out where you might be, and he had a general idea—at the very least, he knew they were on the east side of the mountain, whereas they'd camped on the southwest side. But that was about all he could tell.

Excited with his newfound powers, he concentrated on the air around him. Can I create a cloud that rains?

He focused and "asked" the air to constrict. It did, and a small cloud formed. He drew from his internal strength and a tiny bit of rain fell from it. He laughed in delight. This was going to be fun!

By the time he made it back to Theo and Amber, they were just waking up.

"Good morning," Basil said. "Can you believe it? We survived trolls and a cave! What a crazy night!"

Theo nodded. "It's amazing to think. And honestly, I

don't think you'd have convinced me to come on this crazy adventure if I'd known we were going to run into trolls. But then again . . ." He looked wistfully up and focused, trying to find any nearby animals. "I never knew I was special. That I had powers."

"That's it!" Amber instantly grew alert.

"What?" Theo looked at her quizzically.

"The pixies back in Seabrook told me I'm special. I bet this is what they were talking about. Don't you think?"

"I don't know." Theo scratched his head, letting a wisp of blond hair trail into his eyes. "I know pixies are magical, but can they know things like that?"

"I don't know." Amber said. "But I've seen them use wands and heal someone. Sage seemed to know we had powers. They probably have the same thing going on. I've always thought they knew a lot—way more than they ever tell us humans. I wonder what else they didn't tell me."

"Well, I can tell you one thing." Basil stood and pointed to the southwest. "We need to find our horses, or we're hopeless here. Amber, the amulet is there, right? Plus your cloak and all our other gear."

Amber sighed. "Yeah, you're right. We need to go back. But what if the trolls are still there?"

"I don't know. But let's start with the horses. I figure our camp is that way. The horses might be long gone by now, whether killed by the trolls or not. But I'm sure our gear will still be there—trolls aren't like goblins. They don't take things . . . they just eat them. So we need to find the horses. Theo, can you figure out where they are?"

Theo closed his eyes and scanned the mountain in his mind. "Nope. Let's start walking."

Basil's experience in the outdoors kept them pointed in a steady direction, and Theo kept on the alert to find their hawk friend. Amber focused on the trees and plants, but that didn't seem to make much difference.

They traveled for about half an hour, with Theo pausing every once in a while. Finally, he smiled. "I found our hawk friend from yesterday! I'm asking her now where the horses are."

He stood with eyes glazed, staring at the clouds. "I know where the horses are! All three are still alive. They may even be where we left them. But they're way over there." He pointed down the mountain. "And I think . . . I'm not sure, but I think the trolls are there too."

Chapter 20

The Trouble with Trolls

"CAN YOU SENSE TROLLS TOO?" Amber asked.

"Not very well," Theo replied. "Regular animals are much easier. But the horses are definitely upset, and I'm fairly certain the trolls are sleeping nearby—probably just inside the cave. They don't like daylight, right?"

"I don't think so." Basil pulled his sword out a bit. It was slightly glowing. "Goblins and trolls are similar in that way, as far as I can remember. Regardless, at least now *we're* the ones sneaking up on *them*, instead of the other way around." He started hiking down the mountain in the direction Theo had pointed.

"Yes, but we need a plan." Amber twirled her hair in thought. "We can't just go in there—the only effective weapon we have is an enchanted sword that seems pretty puny. We've got to figure out another way to stop them."

"Do you think the amulet would help?" Theo asked.

"Maybe," Amber replied. "But it's in one of my saddlebags."

"Even so," Basil said, "I doubt it. It's for lifting the spell, which would help with something like the phoenix, but trolls are big ugly buggers no matter what. Spell or no spell."

"Yeah, I think you're right." Theo pursed his lips and looked around. "We need another plan."

Basil walked back to them and put his fists on his hips. "Since they're sleeping inside the tunnel, we could try to cave it in."

"How?" Theo asked.

"Um . . ." Basil scratched his head.

"Do either of you know why they don't like daylight?" Amber asked. "Would it hurt them?"

Theo and Basil shook their heads. Basil shrugged. "Well, maybe the best we can do is sneak in, get our horses and stuff, and get out of there as fast as possible."

"That could work . . ." Theo frowned. "But remember what Sage told us our mission was? To stop creatures like these from doing more harm. We can't just let them go and kill the next people they find."

"True. But what good is trying to do something against trolls and getting killed ourselves?" Amber asked. "You saw them last night. They're unstoppable. We certainly can't do anything about them. Besides, they're way out here in the wilderness. There's nobody around for miles."

"For now," Theo said. "Mark my words. I think if we leave this opportunity to take out two sleeping trolls, we may never have it again—and may come to regret it."

Amber sighed. "You're right, Theo. But what do we do? Sage didn't give us a lot of advice."

They continued walking and came around a rocky outcropping. Their horses were tied to the trees where they'd left them, down the mountain. They looked skittish and upset.

"Sage taught us to play Castles," Basil said wryly.

Theo grinned. "You're right. There's nothing obvious in one move. But maybe four moves ahead?"

"Well, can you at least calm the horses, Theo?" Basil asked.

Theo nodded. "I hadn't thought of that. Duh. For sure." He focused on the horses and immediately they calmed down. "Okay. Now what?"

"We need to think of this differently," Amber said. "A wise man once told me if you can't figure something out with your first approach, try rephrasing the question. So rather than asking *how do we take out three sleeping trolls*, let's ask something else."

"Like what?" Basil asked.

"Well, how about, what can we do with sleeping trolls? No, that's not it." Amber looked up in thought.

Theo perked up. "What effect can three kids with powers have on trolls?"

"Better," Basil said. They all sat in silence, then Basil looked over at Amber. "I have an idea."

The three crept to their horses and gear. Theo made sure the horses kept quiet by calming them with his powers. Amber went to some trees with big, strong branches and asked them to release branches. One by one, three sturdy and healthy branches broke themselves off the tree and dropped into her hands.

She silently thanked the tree for its gift and reshaped them to shed the twigs, so they were easy to carry. Then the trio walked over to the cave entrance, holding one large branch each.

"Ready?" Basil put his hand on Amber's shoulder as they stood at the entrance.

She looked him in the eyes and breathed deeply. "As ready as I can be, I think."

Theo glanced at her nervously. "Well, it's not like our lives are depending on it, right?" He laughed weakly.

"As long as they don't wake up, this should work," Amber said.

"We're trusting you on this one," Theo said uncertainly.

Basil hugged Theo's shoulder. "She's got this. Let's go."

With Basil leading the way, the trio stepped inside the cave and journeyed deeper into the tunnel. They arrived at the split and went the same way they'd gone the night before, toward the faint sounds. As they got nearer, they heard the heavy breathing and occasional snore from the two massive trolls. They were sleeping next to each other in a wide area, somewhat smoother and more well-worn than the other parts of the cave.

The three friends slowly tiptoed into the cave and each set a branch down next to the trolls as quietly as possible. Theo's branch scuffed a stalagmite and one of the trolls snorted and stirred.

The three froze. The troll grunted slightly and shifted. They watched with held breath until it stopped moving. Theo quietly released his breath and set his branch down, then carefully stepped back next to the others.

Amber focused on the branches. Grow, branches! Grow into big prisons! She poured her energy into them, and they started to curl and wind around the trolls. The branches burrowed into the ground to form roots and wound around and around the sleeping creatures—gently so as not to wake them. Theo snuck behind a rock nearer the entrance, and Basil stood next to Amber, his hand on his sword's hilt.

The trolls continued to sleep through the winding branch prison, and although Amber grew more and more tired, she felt the branches could grow limitlessly, so she continued.

When the branch prison finally covered both trolls, she began making the branches thicker and thicker. The minutes passed. She grew so weary that she staggered.

Basil saw her and reached over, holding her up. He whispered, "How can I help?"

"I don't know. I'm feeling so tired. But I want to make sure they can't break out."

Basil nodded, and Amber leaned on him more while growing the branches as well as she could. The branches grew thicker and stronger until finally she stopped.

"Done?"

"No. Just resting."

Theo half-whispered from his rock. "Maybe try putting your hands on the branches."

Amber nodded. "Thanks. I'll try."

She reached over and touched the branches. Where her hands touched the branches, they grew thicker and stronger, becoming almost as thick as trees.

"It's helping! Thanks for the idea, Theo."

After the branches around the first troll were as large and thick as a tree, Amber moved on to the second troll.

About an hour into the process, she reached a hand up, and Basil helped her to her feet. He walked her to the cave entrance, and they all turned to look at her handiwork.

The trolls were completely encased in massive tree prisons.

"Are they dead?" Basil asked.

"I don't think so," Amber said, exhausted. "But if they did live through that, they'll have a *very* hard time getting out."

Basil patted her on the back as they walked back to the fresh air outside. "Think of how hard it was to hurt those trolls with our normal weapons. And you stopped them. If we'd left them free to roam around the countryside, who knows, they could have gone to Mira or one of the other villages around here—and they'd have torn those folks apart. That was awesome."

Amber nodded. "I didn't think it was possible."

Basil helped Amber mount Buttercup, and she slumped in the saddle, leaning into her horse's neck and nearly dozing off immediately.

He looked at her concerned. "Do you want to ride with me instead?"

"Yeah, I think so."

"Ok." He helped her onto Storm, seated behind him. "I know that took a lot out of you, but that was amazing! You took out two awful trolls!"

Theo grinned. "This is only the beginning. Just wait till we get more practice!"

Chapter 21

The Volcano

THE JOURNEY WAS A RUGGED ONE. They weaved down animal paths and across rocky ground, up and down mountains. The underbrush and trees became so thick they couldn't see anything but the forest in front of them.

Theo and Basil dismounted, walking their horses through the dense forest, giving Amber a chance to recover. According to Theo's map, the volcano was close. Late in the afternoon Basil climbed a tree for a better view.

"Smoke!" he shouted down. "And lots of it. I bet it's coming from the volcano. We're not far now."

Amber started feeling her energy return and helped part

some of the thick underbrush with her powers. They came upon a steep incline with crumbly, mossy ground. Basil climbed up, slipping a little, and grabbed at roots to pull himself up, getting twigs and leaves stuck in his hair.

"We made it!" he shouted down with a grin. "The volcano!"

He clambered down and they found another way around. They rounded some large rocks and saw the volcano. Even under their dangerous circumstances, they marveled at its beauty, standing stark and tall next to the sea with a thin plume of smoke coming from its top.

They traveled mostly in silence toward its base, then began their ascent.

"Did Sage say anything about *where* exactly we're supposed to be looking?" Theo asked. Amber and Basil shrugged.

"Maybe we should go to the top?" Amber suggested.

"I can't imagine anything living in hot lava," Basil said.

"Do you have another idea?"

They shook their heads and continued on their way.

The volcano seemed like an ordinary mountain for a while, with grass and scattered trees, but they soon got to a section that was fully dark rock, with all sorts of little holes in it.

Amber examined the rock. "This must be what happens when the lava dries."

Theo ran his hands over the ground. "Yes. It becomes rock. I wonder what causes the holes?"

"Maybe it's because it becomes a rock so quickly." Basil was holding a small stone, inspecting it carefully. "Other rocks are formed underground, but these come straight from lava, right here in the air. This is really light." He tossed the rock a few times, then put it in his pocket. "That would be a good question to ask Chandler."

"If we ever survive this trip to see him again," Theo said sullenly.

As they neared the top, the travelers saw that the smoke at the top was coming from a small source within the large opening. They kept going all the way to the edge and peered down. A steep cliff went straight down on all sides, ending in a rocky basin far below. There was a hole in the middle of the basin with smoke coming out of it.

None of them had ever seen a volcano or a caldera before, and they stared at it in awe for a while. Basil leaned over the edge, then stood again. "I don't think the phoenix lives in there. It's probably in a cave. Maybe somewhere that has access to the heat from the mountain."

They searched for another hour, then turned and went

back the way they came. The view was spectacular, with the sea on their left and the mountainous forests before them. They scanned the mountain for cave openings.

"How on earth will we be able to find a cave on a mountain of this size?" Theo shook his head, discouraged.

Amber and Basil stood silently. None of them had an answer. They waited around, as if hoping the phoenix would suddenly appear. Eventually, Basil started walking again. "Well, let's set up camp somewhere and figure out what to do."

After an hour of meandering along the volcano, they found a spot to camp, much farther downhill. It wasn't ideal but was a bit flatter than the higher sections, and it had trees and bushes to give them some shelter. With food in their bellies, and a small fire to keep them warm, ideas started coming to them.

"We could just sit at the top and watch for it." Amber stared at the embers as they twirled and floated, then disappeared into the night. She whittled a stick with her fishing knife.

Basil shook his head. "Yeah, but we'd have to watch all directions. With only three of us . . . seems like a long shot." He turned to Theo. "You could convince a hawk to fly over the mountain, to find it more quickly."

"I can do that." Theo's eyes glazed over as he searched for animals around them. "I don't think this is the answer, though. Like I said, I don't actually see what they see. And I've lost our hawk friend. We need another idea."

He sighed. "Sage never told you anything else, did he?" They shook their heads. He frowned. "This is foolish. We have nothing to go on. Hoping we find a hawk that happens to lead us to it. This is a big waste of time."

Amber pointed her stick toward the top of the volcano. "Hey. We made it this far, right? Sage believed in us. Maybe we can walk around the volcano and watch Basil's sword. It'll glow when it's near the phoenix, right?"

Basil shook his head. "I've got to be close for it to work. This is a huge mountain."

"Well . . ." She glanced at Theo, who was watching the fire with his chin resting on his hands. "Let's do both. We might as well walk around the mountain to see what we can see. Use some birds, Theo. And let's look for caves as we walk around."

Theo sighed. Basil patted him on the back. "I get it, Theo. It's not a strong plan. But at least it's a plan. Right?"

"I guess so." Theo shook his head.

"Let's play Castles," Basil said. "Maybe that'll inspire us."

"Sure." Theo stood wearily and brought the game over.

They played a few games, with Theo winning easily. His mood never picked up, and they went to bed unable to come up with better ideas, knowing it could take weeks to search the entire volcano.

The next two days were difficult and grueling. They searched throughout the day for caves, walking around and around the volcano in the hot sun, hoping for a sign of the phoenix or even a reasonable cave.

They found a hawk pretty quickly the first day, but the hawk idea turned out to be as unhelpful as Theo had guessed. What good was a hawk if the phoenix wasn't even there? Maybe it was off burning some other village?

Their food supply was starting to get low, and the hawk hadn't found them any rabbits. They felt themselves growing discouraged.

Basil sighed. "Maybe we should hunt for a bit?"

"Yeah, I'm sick of this dried food." Theo patted his belly. "I don't like the idea of splitting up, but you're a good hunter . . . maybe you could look for some deer? I know I sensed some a couple of days ago on that mountain next to us."

Basil shrugged. "I suppose. What do you think, Amber?"

"I don't know. A deer would be great though. It would

last us more than a few days. Who knows how long we'll be here—if Sage is even right about the phoenix living on this volcano."

Theo shook his head, discouraged. "That's right. He said it was here, but then again, what if it's sort of *near* here, not on the actual mountain?"

"Yeah, you're right." Basil turned to Amber. "Either of us could try our hand at hunting, but at this point, I think one of us should. This could take a while."

They all agreed. Amber thought about her parents and village. She missed them dearly. They were so close to finding the cause of all the trouble. Yet they were stuck wandering around the volcano.

She wondered how far down the coast Seabrook was. She imagined it would only take a couple of days from the volcano. Funny, how nobody at the village ever mentioned there being a volcano this close.

Basil returned from hunting with no fresh food, and Theo grew even more discouraged. Amber breathed deeply, thinking of how to cheer him up. "So tell me, Theo, when did you start finding animals attracted to you?"

"Oh gosh. When I was super young. I guess I don't really know. Because I've always loved animals, and they've always loved me. I just figured it was natural." A small chickadee landed on his shoulder, as if to prove his point.

"Did you ever feel like you could communicate with them before you knew you had a power?"

Theo paused and thought for a moment. "I guess there were a couple of times, but I never thought about it till now. Once I was playing with a cat and wanted it to jump across the room to catch a feather toy. My friend Pender was doing the same thing, but he couldn't do it. I got the cat to do it. I just figured at the time that I was good with animals—not that I was telling it to do stuff with my powers."

"Huh. Curious. I wonder if we're born with these powers or if we get them later?"

"Well, how about you?" Theo asked. "Was there a time you remember having control over plants?"

"No." She shook her head. "I was always just good with them. I could grow plants no one else could, and I could also—sort of—feel their moods. I know that sounds weird, but plants get unhappy too. We'd grow these big crops of food, and I'd say to one of the farmers that the wheat wanted a bit more compost or this crop needed more water and this one less."

"Oh, and here's another thing," she went on. "Did you know certain vegetables like to grow next to each other? Nobody else knew that in my village, but I told them that the beets want to grow next to the garlic, and the broccoli next to the onions. And guess what? They were *way* healthier. All of them! We'd had this snail issue, see, eating all the beets, and when we did that, it just solved it instantly. Plus, they tasted better. So, of course, everyone does that now."

"That's amazing." Theo looked inspired. "How long ago did you do that?"

"Oh, I don't know. It's been a few years now. So, yeah, maybe I've always had these powers. I just didn't realize they were magical."

They chatted into the night, trying to relax, but there was tension in the air. Would they even find the phoenix at all? Was the entire mission impossible from the start?

The next morning Basil took off on foot to the next mountain to hunt while Amber and Theo continued their search. They tried using their powers throughout the day. Amber stretched her mind to find out how far she could sense plants and trees. It was farther than the last time but still not much more than a couple of stone throws away.

She thought about the vivid dream she'd had the night of the trolls. The trees had talked to her.

She tried communicating with the plants around her,

but nothing felt strong and vibrant—nothing like she'd experienced that night. During the waking hours, it was more like she had a sense of things, what sort of moisture and sun they needed. It felt very familiar, like when she was back in Seabrook helping people with their farming decisions.

Theo practiced with animals. He brought different kinds of birds, from hawks to hummingbirds, and sent them around the mountain to get their perspective on where the phoenix might live. Just like his earlier attempts, it didn't bring any results.

On his own, Basil also tried many different things to control the air but couldn't seem to do more than tighten it, push wind currents around, or whip little bits of leaves off the ground. He could create serious gusts of wind when he focused hard but felt like he must be missing something.

And he hadn't found any deer, so that night they felt tired, discouraged, and hungry for fresh food.

On the third day, it started raining, and the search became nearly impossible. Amber's enchanted cape turned out to be waterproof, but Basil and Theo were getting drenched, not to mention their horses and all their gear. They decided to go back to their camp and wait it out.

Basil made a fire at their site, and Amber caused the branches to create a canopy to shield them from the rain. The boys changed clothes and hung their wet clothing out to dry.

Amber felt chilly and pulled out the black-and-yellow striped hat her mom had knitted. It felt like so long ago, and the bright, happy colors seemed so out of place with the grey rocks and rain.

"Hey! Love the hat." Basil smirked. "How come you haven't worn that before?"

Amber pushed a strand of hair out of her eyes and under the hat. "There's a pixie that would be losing a bet right now."

"Huh?" Basil looked at her, puzzled, and Amber laughed.

"It's not just for looks. It's a nice, warm hat."

"Okay." Basil shrugged and turned back to lighting the kindling he'd set up in the ring of rocks.

The fire quickly warmed them to their core. Basil whittled a stick with a knife, and Amber found herself getting entranced by the dancing flames. Theo pulled out a small book.

"What are you reading, Theo?" Amber asked.

"This?" Theo looked at the book sheepishly. "It's a book of short stories."

"Neat." Amber peered at the cover. "I only brought one book with me. It's a great story about elves and a dragon. I'd have brought more, but I didn't know how long I'd be gone.

I have some great books back home."

"I bet," Theo said. "Do you have a library or some place to read more books in your town?"

"Naw. But there's an old woman, Mrs. Juniper, who has quite a few. I like to go over to her place and read, or she sometimes lets me borrow them. We don't really have any place like Chandler's in Seabrook."

Theo put his book down. "I can't imagine life without a library or a teacher. Is there a school there?"

"Not really. Mrs. Juniper teaches lots of folks to read— including me and my brothers and sister. But no, I'd say only half the folks in town really know how. We spend a lot of time working outdoors. My parents read at night, so I grew up with them reading to me, and I learned pretty young. But a lot of folks don't have that."

Theo nodded. "Sounds like there's not a lot to choose from. Did you learn much history or science?"

Amber thought about it for a bit. "Some, I guess. A lot of it is passed down around the fireplace. My dad likes to tell stories, and he thinks it's important to remember things from the past, so I know a bit. But not like Chandler. I couldn't believe how much he knew about everything."

"Yeah, he's a bit of a know-it-all," Theo said.

Basil interrupted, "You can say that again! He's totally

full of himself. Thinks he knows everything. But then, I guess he *does* know a lot. He's helped out the folks of Sanford more times than I can count, so they treat him with respect."

Amber poked the fire with a stick. "I never thought about how knowing history could be so helpful, but I got a glimpse of it back at Chandler's place. Before we even found Sage, it's like we figured out all sorts of stuff. And the maps! I've never seen maps of the land like that before. I guess, besides hearing Ryder's stories, I hadn't really thought about how far the land goes."

Theo nodded. "Yeah, it's pretty great having that kind of knowledge. I really want to learn more. I hear Lugo has a huge library. I'd love to visit it someday."

"Sounds like a great idea," Amber said.

The rain continued all day and into the evening, so they didn't bother leaving their campsite. They played Castles, and Theo showed Basil and Amber some of the strategies he'd worked on. Amber was impressed at how many levels of thinking could be added to such a simple game.

Basil left for a while to set up a few rabbit traps, but when he checked them at the end of the day, there was nothing. The three went to bed once again with a meager dinner of jerky and the last of their stale bread. The next morning, the search continued, and Amber wondered if they'd all have to hunt for more food.

Then, that afternoon, with no warning, the phoenix appeared far below them and flew away down the coast.

It was an unbelievably fierce-looking creature, like an oversized yellow, orange, and red eagle with glistening scales and a long reptilian tail. It appeared massive and foreboding, even at their great distance from it.

Amber felt chills go down her body. How would they get close to a creature of that power? She realized it was flying down the coast toward her village. She hoped it wasn't going to burn another field. Or worse yet, attack the villagers.

"We need to get to that cave before it gets back!" Basil said excitedly.

Amber shook her head to focus, and the three scrambled down the mountain face, toward where they thought the phoenix had been. Even knowing the general area, they had no clue where to look. The cave was perfectly hidden.

Suddenly, Theo's face lit up. "Rats!"

"Come again?" Basil said.

"There are rats over there. Come on!"

They clambered across the rough terrain past trees and long grasses and over large rocks, then came across a small opening between the rocks. Theo focused, and instantly a dozen large rats came pouring out of the hole. Amber had to keep herself from jumping up and running away. The rats stood in front of Theo, as if taking orders from him, then dispersed in every direction.

Theo flashed a smile. "We'll find it in no time now."

Sure enough, only twenty minutes later Theo called, "This way!"

They ran and climbed over the rough land and came upon a large cave opening.

"There's no way we'd have found this," Theo said, peering around a rock. The cave was completely hidden from nearly every angle, and they wouldn't have realized it was there, even if they'd walked right up to it.

"What's our plan?" Amber asked, looking at her friends.

"Let's go in and see." Basil held the hilt of his enchanted sword tightly.

The cave entrance might have been small, but inside it was enormous, with craggy spots all around and all sorts of rocks and crevices. Sunlight filtered down through a small hole into the lofty space, making the entire place feel magical. It was mostly empty, except for a large padded nest of grasses and numerous bones scattered about. It had an unusual sculpted look, as if it had been burned and melted over the years to suit the phoenix's needs.

"Look." Basil pointed behind the nest. "That rock there

is large enough for you to hide behind, and it's right next to the nest. Here's what we can do. You hide there with your cloak and the amulet. Theo and I can hide behind these other rocks over here. When it gets close enough, leap from the top of the rock onto its head and drop the amulet over its neck. If it gets wind of you, Theo and I can distract it.

Amber gulped and nodded. They all hugged each other, then hid behind different rocks, waiting.

Time passed slowly, and nobody said a word. Amber sat holding the amulet in her hands, turning it over and over. Maybe we won't die today, she thought. To prepare herself, she slowed her breath, focused, and imagined how she'd leap onto the phoenix at the right moment.

But when the phoenix returned—its huge fierce body landing quietly on the cave entrance holding a deer in its talons—Amber grew pale. Her hands trembled as she held the amulet and listened to the large creature tear into its prey. She closed her eyes and took a deep breath. Would she be able to do it?

Chapter 22

Pixie Power

FLURRY HID INSIDE THE SMALL HOLLOW OF A TREE, holding tightly onto Wix. They sat in the far back corner in the shadows and listened intently. The forest was eerily quiet.

A pixie mind-spoke to the general area: *Three imps. Maybe four. At least ten of us dead. Stay hidden. The elders have a plan.*

The fact that the elders had a plan was somewhat comforting. But not really. There was no question in Flurry's mind at this point. They *had* to get to the Great Stone Tower. I wonder who's dead, she thought. Then she shook the thought from her mind. No time for that now. Survival depended on being fully present.

Time felt like it slowed down. They waited and waited. When would they know if the imps were gone? All of their usual senses to detect living creatures seemed useless. She tried listening, but it was futile inside the tree.

After what felt like hours, the pixie mind-spoke again: *There were four imps. They've passed us now. Let's regroup at the cherry blossom tree we saw back by the ring.*

Flurry and Wix peeked out of their hole. No other pixies were visible. They darted into the open and sped toward the tree. It was in full bloom, with pink-and-white blossoms covering every branch and filling the whole area with a sweet smell. Twenty other pixies hovered, glancing around furtively. Flurry was heartbroken to see so few, especially since she only recognized half of them.

One of the elders raised his hands and mind-spoke to them: *The ring nearby can be restored with minimal magic. We can use it to cast protective spells and have a safe night, invisible to the world. From there we can devise our next plan. We know we need to get to the Great Stone Tower. But it's far. We must deal with the imps first.*

All the pixies silently agreed. A few stayed behind to communicate with any stragglers still arriving, and the rest flew over to the mushroom ring. It was old and incomplete—

but nothing a few spells wouldn't help.

The pixies with power over plants worked quickly, as did the mages with their wands to enchant the ring. In short order, the whole area began to shimmer, and golden sparkles appeared, rising up from the mushrooms and creating a dome around the fairies.

As the minutes passed, the sparkles grew thicker and thicker, until finally all the pixies relaxed. They were invisible to the outside world now. More pixies continued to stream in through the walls, adding to their numbers. Flurry felt comforted that there were more than the original twenty that had shown up at the blossom tree.

The regal-looking male elder called them in, then stood in front of the group. "How many tribes are represented here?"

Two elders from different tribes flew over to the speaking elder and stood next to him. One pixie looked around frantically, then flew over too but looked discouraged. Not an elder by any stretch but representing her tribe. Four tribes in all were present.

As a few more streamed in, Flurry did a quick estimate—about seventy pixies were present. That meant over a hundred had been separated from them or killed in the last week. She shook her head and tried not to cry.

The elder spoke again. "The fires have been targeted all along the sea, but there are still many more tribes down the coastline. No tribe has been prepared for this. We can't count on them to solve this issue. We may not be able to prevent the fires, but we *can* come up with a strategy against the imps. Are there any pixies here with the power of illusion?"

One young pixie raised her hand and flew over to the elder. "Yes. But I was a student. Not a full-fledged mage."

The elder continued. "You can show me your limits shortly. Any pixies here with elemental powers?"

Flurry and two other pixies darted forward, next to the elder. "Your powers?"

"Earth." Flurry nodded.

"Plants," said the other two.

The five younger pixies and three elders hovered above the rest. "And finally, any pixies who are strategic—who think they can help us devise our plan. Come forward now."

There was an awkward pause. A middle-aged pixie looked around at the others, then flew up to the group. Another one quickly followed her lead.

Dismissed, the elder mind-spoke, wiping his hands. The rest of the pixies relaxed. Flurry and the other nine pixies flew to a rock and landed.

"At this point, we have a very simple plan. We'll fool the

imps into thinking we are elsewhere, then sneak attack them. Since our normal powers don't work on them, we'll have to use the elements around us—earth, plants, and whatever else we can come up with. We have the perfect place for a sneak attack in mind . . . it's a narrow valley with lots of rocks to hide behind." She looked at Flurry meaningfully. "Or hurl."

Flurry gulped and glanced around at the others nervously. Her role would be critical to the plans.

"Any other ideas, please share them now."

A moment passed, then the first pixie, a kind-looking woman, spoke up. "We need to consider how to better use our power over plants. The imps are far too fast to be caught in woodland prisons, but I've seen arrows created from thrown branches, and I've seen arrows themselves become more effective under guidance. Depending on the skill levels present, we could have pixies line up on both sides of the valley. We can create large crossbows to send arrows toward the imps—as long as they are fooled into thinking we are in a certain spot." She glanced at the young pixie who said she could create illusions.

"I . . . can . . . do . . . it," she said, then closed her eyes and breathed in deeply for a moment. "I've done illusions that size before. Just not for a long time. We'll have to be precise about when they're nearby, so I can limit how long I have to keep up the illusion."

Flurry cleared her throat. "Perhaps we could make it look like only a few pixies are there, so it's easier? I'm sure the imps would attack, even if they only saw three."

"Indeed," the elder nodded approvingly. "The key is having all four imps together at the same time. That may be our greatest challenge. I'm not sure an illusion will do it. We may need a real pixie to draw them in."

The second pixie who volunteered for strategic thinking spoke. "We developed a system in our tribe to lure them away and then hide. We figured out they somehow are able to sense us—but only when we're flying. If we're on the ground or in trees, they're as blind to us as any creature."

"Really?" The elder raised her eyebrows.

"Yes. What we did is show ourselves near a good hiding spot, then lure them away from the larger group and stay hidden till they were long past. I'm guessing most of my tribe are still on their way to the Great Stone Tower now. I was one of a few who took on the role of luring them in the other direction."

"Then it's settled. We'll get our fastest pixies to lure them into the trap. Those in the valley will remain hidden and not fly at all. The illusion will show three pixies flying through the valley, somewhat slower than normal. And we'll attack them with crossbows and hurl rocks—or even create an avalanche if need be—as long as we're protected."

She wiped her hands, and all the pixies immediately got to work.

The bows took the longest time to build, but thanks to the pixies with power over plants, the group had four large crossbows within an hour. Flurry flew to the valley with a dozen other pixies to scope out the area. There were some large rocks above, and she imagined having them rise from the ground and go flying toward targets below. The imps might see them coming, and they were quite fast, but she still thought she had a good chance.

The pixies all found hiding spots behind rocks and tree branches, then stopped flying. And waited. Over a dozen pixies had been sent to lure the imps their way. Flurry hoped they were okay.

The day waned, and the sun grew warm. It would have felt like a beautiful day, if not for the imminent danger.

All at once, a pixie mind-spoke to all the pixies in the area: *Three imps coming.*

The illusion of three pixies standing in the middle of the valley suddenly appeared. They weren't flying in the illusion, so the imps wouldn't be keyed into the fact that they couldn't sense them.

A moment later, two imps zipped into the valley. Their intensity and speed were startling, even to the pixies who'd seen imps before. They lunged toward the pixies in the illusion, and the fake pixies scattered and hid under the rocks. The third imp remained unseen, and Flurry was unsure whether to wait or attack.

Her mind raced and imagined a dozen options in a matter of seconds. The imps are distracted. It's now or never.

She focused on loosening the largest rocks directly above the imps and sent them rolling down the hill. They gathered other rocks and dirt on the way, creating a landslide. As expected, it was near impossible to guide them once they'd left the earth, but thankfully she had sent them hurtling in the right direction.

Now, she thought, I just hope the imps don't see them.

Thankfully, the imps had scrambled onto the rocks and dug their claws into the holes where the illusion pixies had gone. They screeched oddly, like injured birds.

Flurry kept her focus on the rocks, then switched her focus to the imps. One of them had its hand deep in a hole, and she caused the rocks around it to close in, trapping it. It squawked and tried pulling its arm out. The other imp looked up at it with a quizzical expression, then the rocks hit.

The two imps were buried in the landslide, covered in five feet of rocks and dirt. The rocks settled, and the dust flew into the air, obscuring the entire area.

The pixies all waited in silence.

Flurry focused on the entrance to the valley where they'd come from. The trees were thick there. She mind-spoke: *Where's the third?*

Still here. Watching, a pixie replied from the woods. Flurry could sense he was just at the edge of the trees. He continued: *It looks like it's smelling the air. Nobody fly.*

The sun beamed down, warming the earth. The pixies without shade shifted and wiped sweat off their brows—but never left their crossbows. Hours passed, and the sun finally dipped lower in the sky.

Flurry's mind wandered. How many imps were still after them? Besides the two in the area, of course.

Vibrant rose colors filled the area as the sun set. However beautiful, the wait was painful, and the valley grew darker and darker.

One of the pixies in the valley mind-spoke to everyone: *Is it still there? Should we do something? We won't be able to see it soon. I know they see better in the dark than we do.*

Flurry replied: *Yes. It's still in the same spot.*

The other pixie continued: *I think it's going to wait until one of us moves or flies. If I risk it, you'll have to be fast.*

Even in mind-speak, Flurry could tell the pixie was nervous. Then she had an idea: *Can you get ahead of it, coming toward us? You've seen how fast they are. Can you outpace it?*

There was a pause as the pixie thought about it: *No. I don't think so. Maybe we can make an illusion. I'll fly as fast as I can toward you. When it's close, I'll stop flying and drop from the sky. If you can hide me as well as possible at that point and make it look like I'm still flying, we can lead it to the crossbows.*

Silence rang out in the darkening valley. Then the first pixie mind-spoke again: *This will only work if it's true about them not seeing us when we're not flying. And you'll have to risk hitting the ground—that could kill you. But you'll need to wait to fly till the last minute.*

There was an awkward pause, then the pixie closest to the imps replied: *Understood. Is everyone ready?*

A chorus of pixies mind-spoke. All were prepared. The pixie suddenly darted from the trees toward the valley, the imp instantly behind it with ferocious animosity. The pixie was still far from the ambush when it shimmered briefly, then appeared to speed up. The illusion was convincing—it did appear to be the same pixie flying.

Puzzled, the imp faltered for a moment, then squawked and dove toward the illusion. Just as it was about to grasp it, the arrows flew, two from each side of the valley. The pixies with plant powers focused all their might, and one of the arrows hit the imp solidly right through the chest. It gave a startled gurgle and dropped to the ground.

We did it! A chorus of pixies rang out. They emerged from their hiding spots and stretched their limbs and wings, then fluttered together at the center of the valley to ensure everyone was present. The moon rose, casting a beautiful glow over them. All had survived. They had defeated three imps.

Flurry felt her heart lift. With their new knowledge of the imps, and working together, it definitely seemed possible to make it to the Great Stone Tower. She thought of the friends and family she hoped to see again. And how they could use the power of the tower to learn more and deal with the attacks properly. She'd never been there before, but it was legendary—a strong source of mana.

It might take weeks to get there, but she would try. The biggest challenge, in her eyes, were the fires. They had no way of dealing with fires. Something had to be done to stop them . . . and soon. Or the pixies would be killed all along the sea.

For a brief moment, she wondered what Amber was doing. Could she help stop the fires? Has she discovered her special powers yet?

Chapter 23

Phoenix Rising

THE PHOENIX TORE INTO THE DEER CARCASS with its massive beak, pulling the fur off and eating the meat beneath. Amber, Theo, and Basil crouched behind large rocks scattered around the cave, afraid to show themselves even the tiniest bit. The smell of blood filled the spacious cave.

The enormous orange-and-red body rippled with muscles, and they could feel heat coming from its body, as if it could burst into flames at a moment's notice. The phoenix's body was covered in both scales and feathers, part lizard, part bird. Its beak was sharp and curved like an eagle's, and covered in blood.

Amber had a flashback to seeing an owl tear into a mouse once, and this felt very similar, only on a completely different scale. The deer, and all of the youths in the cave, were incredibly puny compared to the massive creature.

The light from above created scary, stark shadows on the gruesome dinner. The sound of the phoenix tearing into the flesh echoed around the cave, and the three imagined their bodies being next. Theo steadied himself and took a deep breath, the image of being eaten alive ingrained in his mind.

Before the phoenix had finished eating, they heard loud flapping from outside the cave. The phoenix raised its head and stood. Was there *another* phoenix they had to deal with?

The trio watched from their hiding spots, trying to stay as invisible as possible. A large creature landed at the cave entrance and walked inside. It had the backside of a brown horse and the frontside of a gigantic golden eagle. Its beak and front claws looked incredibly sharp, menacing, and powerful.

But what was even more scary was the man who was riding it.

He was encased in sinister darkness and wore all black—tall boots, riding pants, leather armor, long gloves, and a flowing black cape. He had a large beard and a scowling spirit about him that seemed to emanate evil. He had a short sword on one side, a wand tucked into his belt, and a silver rod in a holster, strapped to his other side.

As the trio watched him dismount from the flying creature, they all thought the same thing: this most definitely is an evil wizard.

The dilemma of their situation began to sink in. They were three kids stuck hiding in the cave of an already fearsome beast and now joined by a powerful wizard and his imposing steed, a hippogriff.

None of them dared move even an inch for fear of making the slightest noise.

The wizard strode over to the phoenix, pulled the scepter off his side, and held it up. It was elegantly designed— a dull, smooth metal that seemed agile and light with a simple, somewhat curvy shape. The top was ornate, with a bulbous spot to hold a small stone that shimmered purple when it reflected the light.

"It is time," the man said in a bold voice, "to attack the next village." The tip of the scepter glowed purple briefly, and the phoenix calmly watched the man with alert eyes. "Go at dusk to Port Turnwater and burn it down."

The phoenix gave a slight nod of its head, and the man nodded at the same time, then put the scepter back into its holster. The man's scowl turned into a nasty smile. He turned, walked to his hippogriff, mounted it, and flew away. And just like that, he was gone. The phoenix stood for a moment more, then went back to eating its deer, as if nothing had happened.

Amber's heart raced. The pure fear the wizard had brought into the room stayed with her. She was already so scared of what the phoenix could do to her. But this was a different challenge altogether.

Maybe we just need to leave, she thought. We're way out of our element here. We have no idea what we're doing.

She tried figuring out how to communicate to Basil and Theo that she no longer felt ready to do the plan. They *couldn't* do it! How could they? She needed more time to figure out a better solution.

The phoenix finished eating and walked over to its nest, near the rock where Amber hid clenching her fists and trying to feel invisible. It turned in a circle and lay down. Amber kept crouched behind the rock, thinking of ways to escape. She wondered how long before the phoenix would smell her and kill her.

Her legs were getting extremely uncomfortable, and she felt like she had to change positions. Don't move! she told herself. But it seemed like the phoenix was going to sleep. Maybe it would sleep, and she could creep out?

Time passed, and her leg started to tingle—pain stabbed at her, and she could no longer ignore it. She moved slowly, trying hard not to make any noise, but as she adjusted her leg, she scraped the cave floor slightly.

The phoenix lifted its head abruptly. It turned toward the rock she was hiding behind.

Oh no! Amber thought. I'm done for!

"Yaaaaaaah!" Basil came running out from behind his rock yelling, his short sword glowing bright orange.

The phoenix jumped to its feet and turned toward him, letting out a piercing caw. Basil raised his sword above his head to attack.

Amber watched the events unfolding as if in slow motion, then jumped into action. She clambered to the top of the rock, leaping toward the phoenix just as it started to spit fire.

She held the chain of the amulet out in a loop, trying to put it over its head. But it was impossible with the phoenix moving so much. Amber landed on its neck, missing the head completely.

On the positive side, her cape whipped around just as the phoenix's fire flamed toward Basil and landed on the enchanted cape, which doused it instantly.

The phoenix shrieked and shook its head wildly.

Amber held on, the amulet in her right hand. She tried inching the chain up and around the phoenix's neck but couldn't free her hand enough to move it that high. She continued her tight grasp around the neck.

The phoenix continued shaking its head, and it was all Amber could do to keep from being flung across the cave. With the amulet swinging around wildly, she knew she wasn't going to be able to finish her mission.

"Toss it here!" Basil yelled.

Amber was being shaken like a rag but held on to the phoenix's neck while lightening her grip on the amulet enough to release it. The necklace flew out of her hand, across the cave and onto the ground. Basil sheathed his sword, dashing toward the amulet.

The phoenix saw him and spat fire, but Basil instinctively created a wind current that blew the fire just to his right. His arm got slightly singed, but he made it across the cave, scooped up the amulet, and hid behind a rock.

He peeked up.

The phoenix frantically swung its head back and forth, trying to shake off Amber. Basil ran back toward the gigantic scaly bird with the amulet chain opened.

Amber gripped the neck of the phoenix and gritted her teeth. The phoenix spat fire again, but her fluttering cape blocked most of it. The cape smoldered and was hot on her back, but she ignored it, holding on for dear life.

"Caaaaaw!" the phoenix complained and gave an even more intense shake of its head, sending Amber flying across the cave.

Her head collided with the stone wall, and she slumped to the floor, dazed and unmoving. Her head started bleeding, and she saw stars.

The world grew dark.

"Amber!" Theo jumped up from behind his rock and ran over to her. He dragged her behind a nearby rock, out of the phoenix's sight. "Please be ok!" He crouched down and placed his hand with the ring over her head.

With the phoenix still distracted, Basil clambered up the rock behind it. The creature whipped its head around, searching the cave for another target.

Basil took a deep breath and leaped with the chain outstretched.

Out of pure instinct he drew from the internal mana inside and leaped far higher than humanly possible, whipped up by a gust of air.

When the phoenix saw him, it opened its giant beak to attack, but Basil managed to loop the chain partly over its head. A large feathery ruffle at the top made the chain catch.

Basil held on with his left hand and tried jiggling the chain over. The creature jabbed at him, slicing a long gash in his arm.

"Aaaaah!" Basil yelled as his sleeve ripped wide open and blood spattered into his face.

But he kept holding on fiercely and stirred the wind to push him. He swung around the phoenix, feeling the chain cross over the ruffle and drop a bit lower onto the feathers and scales around its neck.

When he was certain the chain had completely surrounded the neck, he let go and dropped to the floor.

In an instant, the phoenix calmed down and looked around, blinking, as if in a daze.

Basil lay on the ground, gripping his left arm and writhing in pain. He rolled around for a moment, then weakly stood and stumbled over to Theo.

Amber blinked her eyes groggily. Theo was blurry but starting to come into focus. She closed her eyes, then looked again. The pain began to subside. She slowly lifted her head. Did they do it? What was going on? She felt confused.

She leaned on Theo and wobbled to her feet, then stood on her own. Theo turned toward Basil, whose arm was gushing blood. He grabbed Basil's arm, putting pressure over it while simultaneously using the ring's healing power.

Basil's face was wracked with pain.

"Please be ok, Basil," Theo pleaded.

He focused, and soon Basil's face went from deep pain to calm. Another minute, and the wound closed over.

Amber shut her eyes, took a breath, and opened them again. "Come on, guys. Let's finish our healing later. We need to do this now."

She grabbed Basil's hand, pulling him to his feet. The three struggled over to the dazed and confused phoenix and stood before it.

Amber cleared her throat. "Hello. I'm Amber. And this is Theo and Basil." She gestured toward her friends. "We're here to help."

The phoenix looked at Amber carefully. She went on. "An evil wizard put a spell on you, and we've just broken it with a special necklace."

The creature looked down at the amulet hanging from the chain around its neck, proving to her that it did indeed understand some of what she was saying, so she went on.

"Under the evil spell, you did some bad things, like burn the fields in my village. But now we could use your help." She took a deep breath. "We'd like you to help us stop the people who put you under the spell. And help with the other creatures they've influenced. We can't do it by ourselves."

The phoenix stood silently for a moment, then let out a piercing shriek.

"Is that a yes or a no?" Theo asked with raised eyebrows and a smile toward his friends.

The phoenix approached Amber, and she inhaled deeply, seeing its large menacing beak come toward her. It proceeded to nuzzle her, and she put out her hand to touch it. Whatever its intentions were before, it was definitely a friendly creature now. She looked at the amulet and wondered about the power in that one small piece of jewelry.

Basil and Theo reached out their hands and touched the phoenix's beak as well. It acted much like their horses, with no intent to do them harm.

"I can't believe we did it." Theo patted its beak and neck.

"Yeah," Basil said wearily. "It's a good thing you've got that ring though. I doubt we'd have survived otherwise. By the way, I'm going to need some more healing in a minute. My arm feels awful."

"Of course." Theo looked at him concerned, then smirked. "Although I don't think the ring can heal your awful handwriting."

Basil let out a chuckle. As soon as the ring was on his arm his face relaxed. Then he smiled wryly. "I wonder if it can heal your awful taste in shirts."

Theo laughed and turned back to petting the large bird. After a few moments, it looked at them expectantly.

"What do you think it wants?" Theo asked.

"Why are you asking us?" Basil said. "You're the one who has the gift with animals!"

"Oh yeah!" He focused for a moment. "It's different from other animals, but I think I can get a sense of things with him. He's a very old, very kind phoenix, really."

"That's good," Amber said. "Although you'd have never known it ten minutes ago!"

"For sure." Theo patted its neck. "I don't think he really remembers much about it. The enchantment, that is."

"Interesting." Basil stretched out his arm. "What do you think it remembers?"

Theo focused again. "I'm not sure. But he still seems confused."

Ambler sidled over. "Hey, Theo, maybe you can use that ring on my head some more. I have a crazy headache."

"You bet." He placed his hand on her head. "So did we finish our quest?" He had a look on his face as if he knew it wasn't true.

"No, Theo," Amber replied. "Think about it. That dark wizard will come back when Port Turnwater isn't burned to the ground. We need another plan—and fast. But what?"

Basil and Theo stood thinking. "Well, we can wait for him here," Basil finally said.

"What?" Amber looked at him incredulously. "He's a powerful wizard! What could *we* possibly do to him?"

"Ok, Ok. You're right." Basil shrugged. "But I don't think stopping the phoenix is going to actually stop whatever they're trying to do. Even if the amulet's spell works forever, that evil guy looked serious. You saw him. I'm sure he'll figure out another way to burn down the coastal towns."

Amber shook her head and looked at the floor. "We can't let that happen. That's my home."

"That's what I'm saying." Basil held his hands out in sympathy. "But I agree, taking on that wizard seems impossible."

They were silent in thought, and the phoenix naturally nuzzled Theo. He instinctively patted it without looking up.

Amber felt torn. "I know we stopped the phoenix, but now we know that wasn't our real enemy. Now that we're this far, I can't leave my family and friends at the mercy of this wizard. But what can we do? He seemed so powerful. With that scepter he used to control the phoenix. And he has a wand. What other stuff can he do?"

Theo pulled his sleeve down. "That's true. We don't know the half of it. Sage said scepters can only do one thing, but I bet with that wand of his he can do a lot more."

Amber sighed and watched the phoenix nuzzle Theo happily. Her eyes lit up. "There *is* something we can do."

Basil and Theo regarded her curiously. "Look, Theo, the phoenix is already your new best friend. You can suggest things to it, maybe it's not a spell like that evil man did, but you said it's nice, right? We have powers. If we have the element of surprise and the phoenix on our side, I think we can surprise the wizard and get the upper hand."

Theo started shaking his head no, but Amber went on. "Theo, we need you. You're the one who mastered Castles. We need some serious strategy right now. Four moves ahead, right? We can do it. We just need to be ultra-prepared."

Theo looked scared, and Basil set his jaw.

"Ok," Theo said reluctantly.

"You've got this." Basil patted his shoulder. "Besides, it's not like our lives depend on it, right?" he smiled jokingly,

Theo rolled his eyes and took a deep breath. He would come up with an idea. And stick it out. Or die trying.

Chapter 24
A Bigger Library

TWO HORSES WALKED down the cobblestone road toward the large city gates. The stone walls were enormous, with turrets every hundred yards and soldiers standing watch at each one. Behind the wall, the city sprawled many stories high in all directions. The two- and three-story houses were mostly made of stones and bricks.

Further in, an enormous awe-inspiring castle stood, with four tall towers rising far above the rest of the city, and red triangular flags with the emblem of a griffin flapping in the wind at their tops. Both men had been there enough times that they paid no heed and continued their discussion.

"What do you mean, epicenter? What does that even mean?" Ryder adjusted his riding hat to block the sun.

Chandler cleared his throat and spoke in a professor-like voice, as if before an entire class. "The theory goes that all mana has its origin in certain spots, like an earthquake that starts at one spot and rumbles outward, getting weaker as it goes."

"So does the mana grow weaker the farther it gets from the epicenter?"

"According to the theory, yes. It does. One of the things I'd like to confirm one day. I'm most certain the library here will have the answers to that, and a great many other things I'm interested in. But what I'm most curious about is what's going on now . . . with the goblins and the phoenix and such."

"Of course." As they continued into the town, Ryder nodded to the soldiers standing guard at the gates.

The bustle of the city was immense. People from every race and region imaginable were busily walking up and down the street, with vendors shouting and selling spices, clothing, supplies, trinkets, gear, and items with unknown uses from their stalls that lined the street.

The crowd instinctively parted as the two horses came through, single file through the busiest of the crowd. They passed the market area to a quieter part of the city, until they reached the enormous library building. It was two stories high, with marble pillars and magnificent steps that led to large double doors.

The windows were ornate stained glass depicting scenes from Lugo's history, many of which included griffins. Larger-than-life statues of great heroes in regal poses surrounded the entire building.

Ryder had walked by the building in the past, but would never have thought to go inside. He cocked his head as he appreciated the intricate artwork, noticing it for the first time.

Chandler watched him with a smile. "First time here?"

Ryder blushed. "No. I just hadn't noticed the details before. So, um . . . Where should we leave our horses?"

"There's a stable around back," Chandler replied, eagerness on his face. He patted his horse to move around to the right to the small building behind it.

When Ryder stepped into the library, he was awestruck. He'd never seen anything like it in all his travels. Books and scrolls lined every wall, from floor to ceiling. The room was enormous, one big open space, with bookcases covering every open spot. Six staircases hugged the walls, and a second floor ringed the four sides, looking down to the main area in the center. The second floor was full of books as well.

The middle of the room had a dozen tables, where a handful of people sat reading or talking quietly. Skylights above cast a perfect light below for reading.

"Whoa. Where do we start?" Ryder gazed at the sea of books—thousands upon thousands. The task of finding any information seemed near impossible.

"There's a catalog system that keeps the books perfectly organized. Every book has its proper place. We simply need to check the catalog to find them."

Ryder followed Chandler to a wide drawer with many labels and small knobs. Chandler pulled out a drawer. It was narrow and deep, filled with small cards with information on them about the books.

"Do you know what you're looking for?" Ryder peered at the cards, seeing they were categorized by title, author, and keyword.

"Yes." Chandler pulled a card out, smiled, and took a piece of paper that was sitting on the top of the drawer and scribbled a note on it, then put the card back and walked toward the bookcases in the back.

Ryder followed him, feeling useless. Chandler pulled a book off the shelf, leafing through the pages for a moment, then handed it to Ryder. "Take this one," he said, looking back at the shelf and pulling out another one. "And this one."

He held the book out without looking, and Ryder fumbled for it.

After pulling off four books, the two walked to a table and Chandler leafed through them.

"What are you looking for?"

"A clue."

"What kind?" Ryder opened one of the books and looked at the title. *Magical Properties of Scepters.*

"Oh, lots of things, actually. Assuming there are actually evil wizards behind all the trouble we've been seeing." He held up his hand and counted on his fingers as he said, "*Who* might be behind this? *What* are they trying to do? *Where* are they possibly located? *Why* are they doing it—like what benefit do they get? And also, *how* might they be planning to do it? We've got all sorts of questions, and I'm certain a lot of the answers are here in this library." Chandler put his nose back in the book and muttered to himself as he flipped through the pages.

Ryder looked at the book in his hands and leafed through it. Scepters seemed interesting, but he had no idea what he would be looking for. He put the book down and wandered around the library. Maybe this wasn't such a great idea after all. He decided to check in at the courier's hostel to see if there was any news from the other couriers.

He walked down the street lost in thought, then turned at the old building where he'd stayed countless times. The hostel was busier than ever, with people of all sorts coming and going, mostly younger men. Ryder walked up to a front desk where a young man, not much older than him, sat and talked with another man who looked like he'd just traveled that day.

"Where were they?" asked the man at the desk.

"Due south of here, at Rueford. Not in the town, mind you, but not far either. The whole town is up in arms. They've started assembling a militia."

Ryder interrupted. "I can't help but overhear. What is it you're talking about?"

The courier regarded Ryder. "Ogres. About a dozen of them. And they're not just hanging back, they're attacking people. Makes a job like ours pretty difficult indeed."

"Have they blocked the road?" Ryder asked.

"Yeah, of course. I think we should send some soldiers from Lugo down. It seems serious. Who should I talk to?"

"I'd go to the barracks," the man at the desk said. "Tonight. Someone there will know what to do."

"Thanks!" The courier nodded and dashed out the door.

Ryder frowned at the man at the desk. "How much of this news are you getting? How bad is it?"

"Worse every day. Mostly I hear about goblin sightings, but that red dragon that people started seeing recently is now coming closer pretty regularly, just south of here, and bothering the townsfolk of the villages. Some trolls have been seen coming further down the mountain than they used to, near the villages in the foothills. And now this."

"Any idea of where they're coming from—maybe one location more than another?" Ryder leaned against the desk.

"I don't know . . ." the young man was lost in thought a moment. "I suppose the stories are from everywhere, but if I had to say one area, I hear a lot of trouble coming from east of here. Like the mountain pass to Ballmore. Seems nobody wants to take that route these days. Goblins everywhere."

"I've been hearing that for weeks. Any news of things past Ballmore?"

"Perhaps." The man tapped the table a minute and gazed at the ceiling. "Yes, there was one person, as I recall. Shoot, I can't remember. It was a month ago, and I was just listening in. I'd try asking around the couriers who usually go out that way. Larry is here . . . he sometimes does that route."

"Thanks." Ryder said. As he walked around the hostel asking everyone he ran into for Larry, he smirked. Chandler may have his ways of finding out things, but I've got mine.

Larry was a dark-haired young man with a slightly patchy beard and weathered clothing, except for brand-new brown riding boots.

"Nice boots!" Ryder said as he walked up.

"Thanks!" Larry looked at them admiringly. "I just bought them. It's amazing what good footwear will do."

Ryder put his hand out. "The name's Ryder. I hear you do the route to Ballmore?"

"That's right," he said, shaking Ryder's hand. "My name's Larry. What are you interested in?"

"I'm trying to learn more about the goblins and other creatures that have been sighted recently. I hear there might be more activity out that way."

"Oh definitely." Larry shook his head. "It's crazy over there. Goblins are gathering all over the place. I've even heard there's a whole gang of them gathering outside. You never see that. Never more than a few at a time, but from what I hear there must be dozens, if not more. Not sure what to think, but the people of Ballmore are definitely not happy. I haven't seen them myself."

"Whereabouts is this happening?"

"Oh, quite a ways east of Ballmore, north toward the mountains. Definitely not close to any towns or anything, but still. Freaky. I've heard that's where the goblins are normally from. The Ancares Mountains. Be careful if you're thinking to head that way."

"Definitely." Ryder paused. "Any other signs of things?"

"I don't know," Larry said apologetically. "But the goblins have always kept to themselves before. So something is definitely up."

Ryder thanked him for his time and walked back to the library. Chandler's nose was still in a book, and Ryder shook his head. Probably hasn't learned anything yet, he imagined.

He cleared his throat. "Any luck?"

Chandler glanced away from his book, and his eyes lit up when he saw Ryder. "Indeed! I think I know where they might be located."

"What? Where?"

"Ah, you see, there's a possibility that they are in the same vicinity as they were in the great Wizard War, which was close to two hundred years ago. The reason I say that is because I believe the goblins are mostly coming from the Ancares Mountains, and that happens to be a mere five miles to the wizards' previous citadel. I would wager that they're still active in that area."

Ryder scratched his head. "I just learned that the goblins seem like they're organizing themselves out in the open in those parts."

"Well then." Chandler paused a moment. "That supports my theory. Or it may. It doesn't actually prove anything, but I think it would be worth sending someone out and investigating if the wizards still have their citadel there. We need to know what exactly is happening out there so we can be ready for it."

The two stared at each other awkwardly for a moment. Ryder felt deep down what he was about to say, before he even thought it. "It's going to be me, isn't it?"

Chandler shrugged, then pushed his glasses up awkwardly. "Well, that's up to you. Of course. I, for one, plan to stay here and read more. I've got a friend I can stay with, and I'm just getting started. This is probably going to take me weeks to find all the answers I'm looking for."

Ryder gazed at the stained-glass windows showing a scene with a man riding a griffin, battling a large three-headed serpent which appeared to be controlled by a wizard behind it. "Well, I do travel a lot. And I can be pretty sneaky if I need to."

He paused, thinking of the wizard in the picture. Something about finding powerful wizards seemed intriguing to him, more than scary. "Ok. I'll do it. Make me a map and highlight the key areas to watch out for. I'll head out tomorrow."

"Excellent!" Chandler clapped his hands. "That will give me enough time to think of all the questions I'll have for you while you're on the ground over there. Do be careful, I'd like you to return and fill me in on all the things you'll learn."

Ryder gulped. He wasn't sure if he was crazy to head straight into the source of the goblins, and potentially the evil wizards, but seeing Amber head out so boldly inspired him. And the thought of meeting a powerful wizard, whichever side they were on, grabbed his interest. Would they know more about his powers and what he was capable of?

He thought of the goblins gathering. Did that mean they were forming an army? That would be bad for everyone. He didn't want to see people suffer from goblins or any other threat. He could do something about it. And he would.

Chapter 25
Magical Strategies

AMBER, THEO, AND BASIL didn't have a lot of ideas of how to counter the powerful dark wizard, so they decided to investigate the surrounding area.

Along the way, Theo talked with the phoenix and visualized the evil man, helping it better understand that it had been under a spell and forced to burn down villages—and that they needed it to fight back.

When he felt the phoenix was going to help them, he scanned the area mentally for other animals. He found some rats and bats and a few snakes but not much else. He gave the different animals a heads-up that he might need them.

Amber found some prickly thorn bushes not too far away and asked them to uproot part of themselves and move their thorns so she could replant them closer to the phoenix's cave entrance. Then she caused them to grow into a small bush. She also found some vines and started a new creeping vine that surrounded the area in front of the cave.

They all worked quickly and efficiently, for fear the dark wizard might come back at any moment. Basil focused on looking for the best location to gain a tactical advantage, depending on where the wizard might land. Theo asked the phoenix how often the wizard would come by, but its memory was blurry. The best they could imagine was that he might return that day or anytime the next week. But the not knowing was unnerving.

"Better to get more food and water now, if possible," Basil said. "The chances are he won't come back tonight, right? We also need to move our horses much farther away, so he doesn't see them. Last time was way too risky."

In the end, they agreed that Basil should take the horses down the mountain into the cover of the trees and also do some hunting again, since Amber's and Theo's powers were critical for their plan to succeed.

The rest of the day passed uneventfully. The phoenix left at one point, and Amber was worried. But Theo said, "He's just going for a little fly around the countryside to keep an eye on things. If he sees the wizard coming, he'll come back right away."

Amber understood—but it didn't make her feel any better about being left alone for the time being. Without the phoenix, they were as good as dead, so Amber and Theo stayed out of view as much as possible.

Basil returned later that afternoon with two rabbits. When it grew dark, they guessed the wizard wouldn't return, so they cooked the rabbits and relaxed, then set up mats and slept out in the woods. They figured if he did return while they were sleeping, their plan wouldn't work, but at least they'd be out of sight.

In the morning they ate more of the rabbits, then packed up their camp gear with their horses and returned to the cave. The phoenix was there and greeted Theo cheerfully. They found hiding spots outside the cave and waited.

About midday, the phoenix, who was sitting outside its cave in the sun, raised its head and stared at the sky. They all turned to look. A speck in the sky was coming toward them. From their hiding spots, the three mentally prepared themselves and waited. Their stomachs were gurgling with fear and anticipation.

A couple of minutes later, the hippogriff came flapping

into the clearing outside the cave, bearing the dark wizard. A fierce, scorching anger covered his face. The phoenix, under Theo's guidance, acted as it had before and stood watching the man arrive.

He dismounted and strode over to the phoenix. "What is the meaning of this?" he demanded.

He pulled the scepter off his waist and raised it when Basil shouted, "Now!" All at once, the three went into action. Theo spurred the phoenix to spit fire at the man, Amber entwined his feet with thorny vines, and Basil shot an arrow at him.

The wizard responded with incredible reflexes. A small tornado erupted around him, causing the arrow and the fire to deflect.

Basil continued shooting arrows, but the wizard had his hands lifted and the whirlwind surrounded him, deflecting the arrows so that they all wobbled elsewhere. It was like he had a magical bubble of air protecting himself.

The phoenix breathed fire again, but it was yet again blocked by the wizard's air funnel. The hippogriff charged and leaped at the phoenix. The two took to the skies, attacking and pecking at each other with their enormous beaks. The phoenix grew brighter and flames appeared all over its body.

The only attack that seemed successful against the wizard was Amber's—a thorny plant twined its way up his legs. Unfortunately, he was wearing black leather pants, and the thorns didn't have the painful effect Amber had hoped. But they did hold him down somewhat.

The wizard turned toward Basil first, since he was shooting arrows, and lifted his hands so that a spiral of wind flew toward him, sending him flying into the trees. Basil crashed into them and disappeared.

The wizard then turned and pointed his wand toward Amber. "Incapacio!" he shouted.

She felt her body turn sluggish. It was hard to move anything, hard to even open her mouth. But her mind still felt sharp. She asked the plants to keep growing around the wizard's legs. It was definitely much easier when she'd had her hands free.

Theo ducked back into his hiding spot behind a rock. He mentally reached out to all the rats and bats he'd found earlier.

The wizard looked around wildly. "I know there's another of you! Where are you?" He tried to lift his legs, but they were stuck by the vines.

He pointed his wand at the vines and shouted, "Bravix!" They immediately withered and died.

Amber felt a pain inside her heart, like a knife jab, sensing their death deeply within her. She reeled, and tears welled up, but she could barely move or cry out because of the spell.

The wizard walked around the area. He glanced toward Basil, still lying battered in the trees, at Amber sitting immobile, and then at Theo's hiding spot. He smiled evilly and strode toward the rock when the air filled with a rushing sound—the sound of many wings flapping and feet scurrying. Hundreds of rats and bats came pouring out toward the man.

"Aaah!" he yelled, then sent a tornado of air toward the bats. Nearly all of them were picked up by the whirlwind and sent flying into the sky. The few left fluttered around his face, distracting him, while a hundred rats crawled up his legs, looking for a place to bite.

Unfortunately, the rats couldn't bite through the man's leather armor. But they did tickle.

"Aah! Ha ha! Stop! Aaaah!" The man laughed and slapped at the rats, wiping them off his arms. There were so many that he couldn't get them all.

With the wizard distracted, Amber used all her will to bring the other vines she'd placed to snake their way over and creep up his legs again. It was utterly exhausting, especially without the use of her arms, but she focused all her inner strength toward it.

The wizard kept whacking at the rats and bats, then lifted his hands and floated, buoyed up by wind currents whirling around him. The rats that fell couldn't get back on, and the wind whirled faster around him, causing most of them to fly off.

Even floating in the air, the wizard had some vines around his legs. They weren't attached to the ground anymore, but Amber felt like she could entwine more of him. So she focused on twining all the way up and around his arms.

Theo continued focusing on the few rats who remained on the wizard and urged the other bats who'd been swept away to return as quickly as possible.

Basil sat up and saw what was going on, then raised his arms and drew deeply on the power he knew was inside him. The wizard suddenly stopped mid-air, halted by the counter-wind from Basil.

"Enough!" the wizard yelled, and a huge gust of wind came whipping through, peeling the rats off his body and causing those on the ground to hold on or be blown away.

The wind buffeted Amber, sending her body a few feet along the earth. She bumped into some rocks painfully. She panicked—would she be injured seriously if she flew into something head-on?

Meanwhile, Basil gripped a tree and tried to create a bubble of safety around himself.

The sky grew dark with thunderclouds and a crackle of thunder echoed down the mountain. The wizard had an evil grin as he flicked the last of the rats off his body and pointed his wand at Basil.

A bolt of lightning flew down from the cloud, onto the wizard's wand and straight toward Basil. It just missed him, jarred by the wind tunnel Basil was creating, and exploded a tree right next to him, sending branches crashing everywhere.

Pieces of bark and branches crashed into Basil painfully. His eyes flashed, and he called out to Amber, "We have to get rid of his wand!"

Amber closed her eyes. The only useful plants she could sense were the last straggling vines still on the wizard's legs. She urged the vines to hurry and climb up his arms. They crept up to the arms and wrapped all around.

Then, a loud shriek pierced the air above them. The hippogriff hurtled toward the ground, completely ablaze, and crashed into a nearby tree. The phoenix followed behind, looking like a ball of flame.

It turned toward the dark wizard and sped toward him.

The wizard partially lifted his wand to point it at the phoenix, but Amber's vines tightened and held his hand down just enough that he couldn't point it directly at the flaming bird.

The phoenix barreled toward the wizard, and with panic in his voice he shouted, "Abrazio!"

The phoenix faltered for a moment, then continued. The wizard tried raising his arm more fully but couldn't. His eyes filled with terror. "Abrazio!" he shouted again.

In an instant, the phoenix powered into him, clutching him in its fiery claws and pulling him into the blaze. The wizard screamed for a moment, and then there was only the sound of fire and flapping as the phoenix flew back up into the air, carrying the dark wizard in the inferno.

Basil stood ruggedly and staggered toward them. Theo finally glimpsed up from behind his big rock and braved standing. Amber still couldn't move, but out of the corner of her eyes, she could follow the phoenix.

The fiery bird flew up, holding onto the wizard, a huge ball of deep red flame that grew brighter and more fierce the higher it went.

Nobody could live through that, Amber thought. Not even a powerful wizard.

Theo crouched down and patted her. "Are you ok?"

She couldn't answer. Her whole body was still completely paralyzed. She grunted slightly. "Uuuuuugh."

His eyes grew wide, and he put his hand with the healing ring on her. Sensation and warmth slowly returned to her body. Her tongue was released, and she breathed in relief.

"Thanks, Theo. It's working." She smiled at him, and he continued to hold his hand on her.

"Hey! We did it!" Basil staggered over, looking happy. "We really did it!" He winced in pain as he limped. Theo gave him a silent look that said, *It's your turn next.*

Basil smiled, despite his obvious suffering. "I think I now understand just how powerful air can be!"

"You've got that right!" said Theo. "That wizard could create lightning and even fly! I wonder if you could do that, Basil?"

"Probably. But who knows?" He limped over to Amber and sat down on the rocks next to her. "But now I get it. He had a lot of effect by creating whirlwinds. He did that the whole time."

Amber slowly sat up. "I bet all of us have the potential of that guy. I wonder how many years it took for him to get that powerful?" She moved her arms around, then stood on wobbly legs.

"Good question." Theo placed his ringed hand over Basil's shoulder, which made him sigh in relief. "I can tell you one thing, though, he really seemed to favor that wand in a totally different way than the scepter he used yesterday on the phoenix."

"Yeah, I wonder what that was about," said Basil. "The scepter is obviously used for enchanting creatures. But that wand . . . he paralyzed Amber, killed vines, and sent the lightning right toward me. Without that phoenix, I doubt we'd have survived."

As if on cue, the phoenix flapped over and landed nearby with a loud thump. The bird's flames were now flickering and going out, but the trio could still feel intense heat coming from it. When the flames died out completely, the phoenix walked over to them.

"Speaking of which," Theo said, "If we want to keep hanging out with this guy, we need to give him a proper name. He's not just an *it*, you know."

"He certainly came in like a blaze of fire," Amber said.

"Let's call him Blazey," Basil said, jokingly.

Amber laughed. "Ok, why not? Hi, Blazey! Welcome back. And thanks for helping us take out that evil wizard."

The phoenix gave Amber a look and cocked his head. Theo laughed. "I'm pretty sure he'd say, 'You're welcome'—

if he could. He seems to understand you. Or some of what you're saying, anyway,"

Basil shook his arm and slowly stood. "Thanks," he said to Theo, then turned to look at Blazey with the others. "So about that scepter—Blazey, do you know where it went?"

Theo focused on the phoenix for a moment. "I think we could find it where he dropped the body. That would probably be our best bet."

"Sounds good." Basil stretched out his arm. "I definitely want to get that back to Sage and figure out what it is. Or maybe we could even try using it ourselves. I don't know. I just don't want us to lose it, in case it's important."

"Get it back to Sage, huh?" Theo looked thoughtful. "So does that mean we haven't finished our adventure? We're not going straight home?"

Basil grinned and looked at Amber. "Maybe not. But yeah, Theo, we did it." He patted Theo on the back. "*You* did it. I knew you could. You're an adventurer after all!"

Theo rolled his eyes. "Well, I did a lot of hiding, it feels like . . . but yeah, I guess so. You guys definitely needed me out here!"

"You can say that again!" Amber's eyes sparkled. "We couldn't have done it without you." She turned to Basil. "I want to go home and see my parents. But I definitely want to get this scepter-thingy to Sage. And something doesn't sit well with me."

"What's that?" asked Theo.

"Well, Sage said there are probably multiple wizards, and we found one. But why was he asking Blazey to attack all the villages by the sea? What's going on with that? And if he's just one of the wizards, will the others pick right up where he left off? Will my village ever be safe until we figure out more and stop all of them?"

"You think we can stop these powerful wizards?" Theo asked.

Basil put his hand on Theo's shoulder. "Well, we *did* just stop one, I'll have you remember."

"Yeah, but it was four against one—if you include Blazey, and we had the element of surprise. How could we possibly take on other wizards who are just as powerful? I don't think I'm up to it, honestly."

"I know, Theo, I know." Basil wrapped his arm around Theo's shoulders. "It's your decision. But we need you. What if we really *are* the kids from the prophecy? Who knows? But if so, well, maybe we'll have an extra bit of luck."

Theo pulled on his sleeve. "Yeah . . . maybe." Then he turned toward the phoenix. "Well, there's one thing I'm extremely curious about with Blazey."

The phoenix walked over to him and put its beak out toward Theo's hand.

"I wonder," Theo said, then paused with a wry smile. "I wonder if Blazey would take us for a ride?"

The phoenix gave Theo a gentle look and lowered his head. Theo grinned and climbed up. After adjusting slightly, he said, "Now what?"

At that moment, Blazey spread his wings and gently lifted into the air.

Theo yelled, "Woohoo!" as he swooped down the mountain riding the phoenix.

Basil chuckled. "Well, I guess that answers *that* question! I call the next ride!"

Amber laughed. "For sure. I'm in no rush."

As the phoenix and his rider glided over the trees and headed toward the sea, Amber couldn't help but feel happy. For the first time in many weeks, she felt hopeful that they might actually succeed in their huge mission.

"I wonder," she said, elbowing Basil in the side, "what that crazy old Sage is going to want us to do next?"

Basil looked up in thought, then smiled.

"What is it?" Amber asked.

Basil raised his eyebrows slyly. "How do you feel about dragons?"

Epilogue

A GRUFF-LOOKING MAN walked up to a woman who was completely white—her clothing, hair, and skin, top to bottom, pure white. The man bowed. "Your majesty."

"Yes?" she replied. "What news?"

"The goblins are almost ready. As well as some of the other creatures you've asked for. Their army is now joined by two other goblin tribes and two sizable giants."

"Excellent," she said. "We'll begin marching on the human cities first. Once the goblins are ready, tell them to march on the human settlements. They should kill anyone on sight and keep their eyes out for brave youths with powers."

"Youths, my queen?"

"Yes. It's that pesky prophecy." She tapped her wand in her other hand. "We must be prepared for all possibilities. But we have many surprises for them. Their efforts will be too little. We're ready this time. Still, if anyone comes across them, send word to me at once."

"Yes, my queen. Any other orders?"

"Indeed. I received word that another scepter has been reported in Somerville. I want you to do everything in your power to bring it to me. Take any resources you need."

"Of course." The man bowed. "And any word from Lucio?"

"No." She shook her head and frowned. "He hasn't reported back for three days, ever since that phoenix failed to burn the next village on the coast."

"Do you think something happened to him?"

"Unlikely," she scoffed. "Lucio can take care of himself." She paused. "But I do need that scepter of his to finish the plan." She turned to the gruff man. "How far along are we on enchanting the army of creatures? I mean, besides the goblins, who are easily manipulated."

"Very far indeed, my queen. We've enchanted nearly all the magical creatures for hundreds of miles. Our army is already strong—it will only continue to grow in strength. We are ready to focus on the next phase of our plan. The good news is that most of the pixies on the coast have fled from the towns, from what we can tell."

"Excellent. And can we find out where the pixies are going?" She stared at him with piercing eyes and a firmly set face.

"Maybe." The man looked uncomfortable. "The general direction—from what we can gather—is they all seem to be headed to the southwest."

"Nothing more than that?" She tapped her fingers together.

"Not yet. But we'll continue to flush them out. One of them is bound to lead us there. Caster remains diligent on their trail with an army of imps."

"Well then," she said, "we will continue as planned, whether Lucio is successful or not. We'll start by sending our army against the largest human cities."

"Yes, my queen." The man bowed.

"And remember, tell all the spies and generals to send word if they find youths with powers. Once we know who they are, they won't stand a chance. Mark my words—this time, it's going to work."

About the Authors

Ephie (dad) has been writing his whole life. Inspired by his sixth-grade teacher to write a story every week, he enrolled in the writing program at his undergrad Middlebury College and has been writing ever since. He loves the outdoors, music, community, his family, and telling stories. He currently lives in beautiful Bozeman, Montana, where he works in software development and is active in various community groups.

Celia (daughter) is an avid book lover and packs a novel with her wherever she goes. She developed the book idea at age nine inspired by a 3rd grade writing assignment. She was born in Vancouver, Canada where her first two syllable word was "hockey"! She, along with her brother, is being raised in the mountains of Montana, where she enjoys sewing, 4H, performance art, and visiting hot springs.

More information on this series can be found at:

theelementalists.net

Acknowledgments

We'd like to thank all the friends and family who helped us make this book a reality. It took *way* longer than we'd thought, and a lot of great people supported us along the way.

If there's one individual to single out, it's Jeff Pernell, who has been a huge support through every step of the process, reading first and later editions, giving a listening ear and advice not just to the storyline but to project planning, publishing and crowd-funding. Thanks, dear friend.

For early revisions, we're indebted to Sam Risho, Jason Crawford, and Tayla Fazio for their feedback that helped turn the book from a kids' short story to a full novel. We'd also like to thank Celia's friends Ella, Analiese, Lily, and Matty for reading and giving their support of a later revision.

We appreciate our cover artist Stephan Martiniere, who did a fantastic job on short notice. And thanks to our inside illustrator Olena Bushana, who went above and beyond to get every scene right and who worked tirelessly on the map.

Special thanks to our developmental editor Ann Castro, who jumped in after we thought the book was nearly finished and turned it from a good story to a work of art. She helped us add layers of depth we hadn't considered. She's read the book all the way through probably five times over the course of ten months, and given advice from over-arching ideas to fixing that final comma.

We launched this book through a crowd-funding effort, and we thank all those who chose to support this book in that way. In particular, special thanks to Joseph Thiebes, Jason Moore, Lance Fisher, Ken, Daniel Lindquist, Taylor Riggle, Arwen & Reuben Cochran, Gary & Kelli Gannon, Timothy Dean, and Arioch Morningstar. We're also thankful to family Tami, Ella, Elia, Eyon, Grandma Alla, and Grandpa Ron.

And of course, this book wouldn't be possible without the loving support of Michelle and Joshua Risho, who sat with us at dinner times listening to our ideas and giving some of their own. They helped in so many ways, especially putting up with us when we disappeared into "story land."

Finally we appreciate you, our readers, for your support. Without you, we wouldn't be able to keep writing. As new authors, you are so important to us, reading, sharing the book with others, and giving us reviews online. Things like that go a long way to help us keep writing.

Author's Note

We were able to publish this book in the way we wanted by self-publishing. During crowd-funding some people picked character names as a part of backing the project. These are the characters who inherited new, better names: Wix, Chandler, Kirsten and Ebeneezer.

Thanks for reading! Please add a short review on Amazon or Goodreads, and let us know what you thought.

To keep up with our progress on the next books in the series, visit theelementalists.net. Coming soon: Book 2 of *The Elementalists series – Crodor the Ancient.*

Till the next adventure!
Ephie & Celia Risho

Don't miss the next exciting adventure in

THE ELEMENTALISTS

Series

CRODOR THE ANCIENT

Chapter 1

An Army of Goblins

THE WIND RUSHED through Amber's hair, whipping it about wildly and stinging her eyes to tears. The dense old-growth forest passed by quickly far below as the massive golden-red phoenix flapped its wings carefully, keeping her from falling off.

As she squinted and tried tucking her hair into her black-and-bright-yellow striped wool hat with one hand, she thought, Next time I ride, maybe a better designed hat and some eye protectors would be a good idea. And a saddle—or something better to hold onto.

She enjoyed the fact that the very phoenix that had burned her village a month earlier was now her friend, giving her a ride over the countryside. In that short span of time, Amber was already thinking about what they could do next to help her people, rather than reading a book at home, which is what she would have been doing before.

They approached tall craggy mountains, and Amber gazed in amazement at the perspective of the land below.

Villages and towns appeared small no matter how large they actually were. A gigantic mountain loomed on her right amidst the vast plains, and just beyond it a city with incredible stone walls and a castle with turrets. Even from that great height, the city was significant. That must be Lugo, she thought.

They circled the city once. Amber was impressed by the sheer number of people and the enormous towers and walls. Then the phoenix turned toward Sage's mountain.

Some dark shapes were moving in the plains to Amber's right, so she patted the phoenix's right side and turned off-course. That was the sign the trio had worked out for letting the bird know where they wanted to go.

The phoenix kept its wings spread, catching a warm air current as it soared over the plains. Amber patted him twice with both hands, and the bird dropped lower, giving her a better look. Goblins!

There were five goblins traveling together, heading with what looked like a strong purpose toward a nearby town. She suddenly had a thought to investigate where they came from and turned directly to the east.

As she flew, she noticed other small groups traveling similarly. It was hard to tell whether they were goblins or not, but she noticed a pattern: they were all coming from a valley in the great mountains to her east, so she continued on.

The terrain changed from plains to foothills, and then to smaller mountains covered in trees. As the trees turned into dense forest it was hard to spot anything, but there was a large road that passed through the valley. Every once in a while she'd see another small group of three to eight traveling the road, much like the ones before.

She kept flying, partly curious and partly afraid of what she might see. The mountains all around at the thick of the pass were steep and snow-capped, then the next ones were shorter again and the terrain turned back into foothills.

As the trees thinned, she noticed a much larger group of moving shapes in an open area. She double-patted the phoenix again and flew in lower.

Close to a hundred goblins were moving together slowly over the plains, headed toward the main road through the mountains. They kept portable canopies above their heads to protect them from the sun.

She dipped even lower to get a closer look. The ugly green creatures were pushing large carts and appeared well organized compared to any of the goblins she'd seen before. Six much taller goblins spread out among them, looking more menacing and powerful—and not as stupid-looking.

One of the taller goblins saw her and shouted something. A goblin grabbed a crossbow, pointed it at her, and let a bolt loose. The phoenix moved abruptly to dodge the bolt, causing her to feel as if she was going to fall. Her heart leaped into her throat and she gripped the phoenix tightly, kicking it with her two feet.

The phoenix flapped its wings and rose up, with more bolts flying after it.

That was close! I can't get that low again. And what were those big, tall goblin-creatures? Not normal goblins, that's for sure.

She felt dread, realizing how difficult that group would be to take on compared to the smaller groups of goblins they'd encountered before.

They rose higher and higher, and then her heart sank as she saw more dark, moving forms in the distance. She squinted, then urged the phoenix to head toward them, dreading what she might see.

As they approached, she frowned.

It can't be. There can't be that many goblins.

Goblins, followed by more goblins, and then more

again. There didn't seem to be an end.

Thousands, Amber thought. There are thousands.

She did some mental math in her head. If there were around a hundred in that first group, then this was about fifty times that size. Five thousand! And it wasn't just goblins. The tall, menacing goblin-creatures were spread throughout—and it looked like two giants in the middle.

She didn't want to get too close this time for more details—but the giants stood at least three times higher than the tall goblins. Probably twenty feet tall.

She circled above them, then tried to figure out how far they were from people. Depending on how fast a large number like that could travel . . . In a few days they could pass through the valley and come across the first villages, and nobody would survive. Then they would get to Lugo. And even a city of that size wouldn't stand a chance.

Three dark creatures rose up from the mob and flapped toward her. She squinted—from her height it was hard to make out, but they were larger than imps and definitely heading her way. Gargoyles, perhaps?

She didn't want to wait around to find out. She lowered her head and turned back toward the north.

As she passed over the thickly forested, mountainous

countryside, she continued to see even more goblins—traveling in smaller groups, less than five.

Then it finally hit her: These aren't just some random goblins. They're scouts.

TO BE CONTINUED